### THE SILKIE

A bullet-shaped living  intense cold and intense h radiation and impacting travel from world to world at astronautic speeds.

### THE SILKIE

A handsome man (or woman) like any other human being, able to transmit and receive thoughts, with an intelligence higher than Einstein's, and yet an emotional flesh-and-blood human.

### THE SILKIE

A fishlike being, able to breathe water and move through the oceans with the ease of a dolphin and the speed of a shark.

### THE SILKIE

Superman? Super-thing? A Frankenstein construction? Computerized demon? Or cunning invader from outer space?

### THE SILKIE

Friend of Earth—or this world's most dangerous foe? Let A.E. Van Vogt tell you the answers in his new novel, a new classic of super-science fiction.

**About the author:**

The magic name of *Van Vogt* conjures up a world of stimulating mental images to those familiar with his works. For A.E. "slan" Vogt is the undisputed Idea Man of the futuristic field.

Canadian born, of Dutch descent, the author is now a transplanted Hollywoodite (although there are those among his legion of fans who secretly suspect his birthplace of being Mars, beyond the stars, or up ahead somewhere, say in the 25th Century).

Van Vogt always is years ahead with his concepts. Semantics, "totipotency," Batesystem vision restoration, hypnotism, "similarization," dianetics, and "Nexialism," have all been grist for his mill.

Author of many best-selling science-fiction books and dozens of short s-f stories, Van Vogt has been repeatedly reprinted here and abroad, translated in French, German and Italian, even recorded on Talking Records for the blind.

Van Vogt speaks fluently the universal languages of excitement and tension, action and invention.

—FORREST J ACKERMAN

# A.E. VAN VOGT
# THE SILKIE

AN ACE BOOK
Ace Publishing Corporation
1120 Avenue of the Americas
New York, N.Y. 10036

THE SILKIE

*Cover art by Jack Gaughan.*

*Available by this author:*

THE FAR-OUT WORLDS OF A.E. VAN VOGT
THE WAR AGAINST THE RULL
THE UNIVERSE MAKER
THE WEAPON MAKERS
QUEST FOR THE FUTURE

# PROLOGUE

## 1

The street of the Haitian city had been excruciatingly hot to Marie's feet, like walking over sheets of heated metal. It was cooler in the garden, but she had to come out from under the shady trees into the sun where the old man sat. Now he laughed unpleasantly, showing his even white false teeth.

He said, "Put up money to raise a sunken treasure ship? Think I'm a fool!"

He laughed again, then blinked his eyes at her with a weary lasciviousness. He added significantly, "Now, of course, if a pretty young thing like you could be nice to an old man . . ."

He waited, sunning himself like a wrinkled toad, soaking the heat into bones that seemed no longer capable of warming themselves. Despite the sun, he shivered as if he were cold.

Marie Lederle studied him with curious eyes. She had been brought up by a sea captain with a lusty sense of humor, and now she was merely surprised that this old lecher could still get a moist gleam in his eye at the sight of a young woman.

She said steadily, "The ship went down during the war near an island off Santa Yuile. It was my father's last command, so when the company refused to sponsor an expedition, he decided to go after private capital. A friend suggested you."

That was a lie; she had made inquiries. He was merely

the latest of a long list of prospects. She went on quickly, "And for heaven's sake, don't get outraged. There are still people who have the adventurous spirit. Why shouldn't an old gambler like you, Mr. Reicher, spend his last days doing something exciting?"

The perfect teeth showed in a grin behind the almost lipless mouth. "There you have the answer, my dear." His tone was more pleasant. "My spare money is going into medical research. I'm still hoping a discovery will be made. . . ." He shrugged his thin shoulders, and naked fear showed on his face. "I don't long for the grave, you know."

For a moment, Marie felt sorry for him. She thought of the time when she, too, would be old and rickety. The thought passed by like a cloud in a summer sky. She had a more pressing problem.

"Then you're not interested?"

"Not in the slightest."

"Not even a little bit?"

"Not even one-tenth of one percent," said Reicher unpleasantly.

She left him with a final, "If you change your mind, you'll find us tied up to pier four in the *Golden Marie*."

She walked back to the harbor, where the small cabin cruiser baked in the sun alongside an uneven row of similar boats. They were mostly seagoing vessels, many of them pleasure craft from the United States. Aboard them were people who played bridge and danced to music from expensive phonographs and lolled in the sun. Marie found herself disliking them because they had ample money and were not like herself and her father, nearly broke and beginning to feel desperate.

She climbed aboard, burning her fingers on the hot wood. Angrily, she slapped her hand against her thigh, stinging the heat pain out of them.

"That you, Marie?" Her father's voice came from somewhere in the bowels of the vessel.

"Yes, George."

"I've got an appointment with a fellow named Sawyer. There'll be quite a few retired bigshots there. One more chance, you know."

Marie said nothing but watched him silently as he came into view. He had on his best uniform, but time had done subtle things to him, and he was no longer the strong, handsome man of her childhood. His temples were gray, and his nose and cheeks were marked indelibly with the wordless trademark of many vintners.

He strode over and kissed her. "I'm hoping particularly to talk to a wealthy old codger—Reicher—who'll be there."

Marie parted her lips to tell him that it would be no use. She changed her mind. She had noticed that his uniform still impressed people. Reicher might not find it so easy to turn down a mature, cultured man.

Not till he had gone did she wonder suddenly what kind of meeting could bring Mr. Reicher out of his hideaway.

She ate a leisurely lunch of fruit from the refrigerator and then composed a poem that sang of the cool delights of the tropical sea where the sun was as hot as a murderer's ire. After filing the poem away in a drawer filled with other bits and pieces of verse, she sat on deck under an awning and watched the sea and the harbor scene around her. The waves glittered in the afternoon sunlight, and reflections sparkled or glared from the white bows of the small craft and from the white walls of the town buildings. It was a scene that still fascinated, but she wasn't sure any more whether she loved it or hated it.

*It's beautiful here,* she thought, *but dangerous for a penniless father and daughter.*

She shuddered at the extent of that danger, then

shrugged defiantly and thought, *At worst I could always do something.*

She wasn't exactly sure what.

She went belowdecks finally and put on her bathing suit, and presently she was paddling around in the warm, gently pulsing sea. The swimming was euthanasia, of course—another day gone the way of a hundred like it, each like a little pebble dropped into the ocean of time, sunk without a trace.

She looked back over that avenue of sun-brightened days, individually delightful, collectively disturbing since she was wasting away her life.

And she was, for the *n*th time, about to make some worthy resolve about her future, when she grew aware that over on the fancy sailing yacht moored a hundred feet away, Sylvia Haskins had come on deck and was beckoning to her.

Dutifully, Marie swam over and climbed wetly and reluctantly aboard. She detested Henry Haskins, Sylvia's husband, so she was relieved when Sylvia said, "Henry has gone to a meeting in connection with a big medical discovery, and we're going out to some island near here to have a look at something or somebody on whom it's been successfully used."

Marie said, "Oh!"

Her picture of Henry Haskins probably differed from his wife's. A cold-blooded bedroom athlete—as described by himself—Henry had several times tried to corner Marie. He had desisted only when confronted with the pointed edge of a knife presented and manipulated with a firmness that convinced him that here was one "crow" he was not going to get.

Henry called women crows, and they pretended that this was a cute way he had of being different. Compared with her husband, Sylvia was mild, friendly, ineffectual, good-hearted—traits made much of by Henry. "Silly is such a good-hearted crow," he would say in a fond tone.

To Marie, the possibility that someone had found a method of prolonging Henry's life was a shuddery idea. But what interested her was the information that he was at a meeting. It seemed instantly certain—in a town the size of Santa Yuile—that it was the same meeting her father had gone to. She said so.

Sylvia exclaimed, "Maybe then it isn't goodbye. I believe Mr. Peddy and old Grayson and the Heintzes and Jimmy Butt and at least two or three others are in on it."

*And old Reicher,* thought Marie. *Oh, my God!*

"Here comes your father now!" said Sylvia.

Captain Lederle saw where she was and stopped. He looked up at the women, rubbing his hands and exuding enthusiasm. "Get my room cleaned up, Marie, as soon as you can. Mr. Reicher is coming aboard this evening, and tomorrow at dawn we leave for Echo Island."

Marie asked no questions before the eager-eared Sylvia Haskins. "Okay, George," she said cheerfully.

She dived back into the water, and presently she was heading belowdecks to her father's cabin.

Her father followed her, and as she turned to look at him, she saw that his happy mood had faded. "We're just hired," he said. "I put that act on for Sylvia."

Marie said nothing, and he evidently construed her silence as an accusation, for he defended himself. "I couldn't help it, honey. I couldn't let even a remote chance go by."

"Tell me the whole story, dear," Marie said soothingly.

Her father was disconsolate. "Oh, some old fraud claims he's got a method of rejuvenation, and these elderly roués are grabbing at the hope. I pretended an interest in the hope of getting something out of it, and I did."

Actually, it was a victory of sorts. From the wreck of his own plans, George had salvaged that magical relationship, further contact. Just what it would mean to have Reicher on board was obscure. But here Reicher would be.

"Do we take along the diving equipment?" she asked matter-of-factly.

"Naturally," said her father.

The thought seemed to cheer him.

## 2

For the sea it was another day of many. The water felt its way with practiced skill among the rocks and coral of that remote island. Here, on the sand backwater, it whispered a soft sound. There, on a reef, it roared at the resistance of the hard rock. But all its noisier emotions were on the surface. In the depths off shore, the ocean was quiet.

Marie sat on the deck of the somewhat dilapidated cruiser and felt at one with the sky, the sea, and the island where the men had gone ashore. She was glad that nobody had suggested bridge for the ladies while they waited for the men to return. It was midafternoon, and the ladies were probably all napping, so she had the ocean universe to herself.

Her idle gaze caught a movement in the water, and she glanced down. And then she leaned forward, gazing downward, startled.

A human figure was swimming far down in the water below her—at least forty feet down.

The sea was singularly transparent, and the sandy bottom was visible. A number of colorful parrot fish wheeled in those crystal-clear depths and sped out of sight into the shadows of the cliffside closer to the shore.

The man was swimming with great ease. But what was amazing was that he was so far down and that, distorted by water movement, his body looked strange, not quite human.

Even as she had that thought, he glanced up, saw her, and swiftly, with enormous power, darted up toward her.

And only then, as he broke free of the sea, did Marie realize . . .

He was not human.

The creature that had come out of the water had a human*like* body. But the skin on his face and elsewhere was unnaturally thick, as if it had fat layers and other barriers against cold and water.

And Marie, who had seen a great many variations in sea life, recognized what was under his arms instantly—*gills*. . . . His feet were webbed, and he was at least seven feet long.

For years now, fear had been her least emotion; so she pulled back a little, shrank inwardly—a little—and held her breath for a few seconds longer than normal.

Because her reactions were that tiny, she was looking at him when he . . . changed.

He was still in the water when it happened. And he was in the act of reaching for the gunwale of her little craft.

The long, strong body shortened; the thick skin grew thin; the head became smaller. Within the space of seconds Marie was aware that his muscles were twisting, writhing, working under a strangely mobile skin. Light reflections and the roiling of the sea obscured some of those motions, but what she saw was a seven-foot "fish" being transformed in a matter of seconds into a completely naked young man.

This being, human in every way, vaulted aboard her craft with effortless strength. He was, she saw, six feet tall and very matter-of-fact. He said in a pleasant baritone, "I'm the person whom all the fuss is about. Old Sawyer has really outdone himself in producing me. But I realize you must be shocked. So get me a pair of trunks, will you?"

Marie didn't move. His face was vaguely familiar to her. Long ago—it seemed long—there had been a young man in her life . . . until she discovered that that she was but one of a dozen girls, with most of whom he carried on a far more exotic existence than she had ever permitted.

This young man looked like that young man.

"You're not—" she said.

He seemed to know what she meant, for he shook his head, smiling. "I promise to be completely faithful," he said.

He continued, "We need—Sawyer and I need—a young woman who will bear my child. We think we can reproduce what I can do, but we have to prove it."

"B-but what you can do is so perfect," Marie protested, only vaguely realizing that she was not resisting his proposal at all. Somehow, she already had a strange feeling of fulfillment as if at last she could do something that would remedy the wasted years.

"You saw only a portion of what I can do," said the young man. "I have three shapes. Sawyer not only reached back into the sea history of man, but he reached forward into its future potentiality. Only one of my shapes is human."

"What's the third?" Marie breathed.

"I'll tell you later," was the reply.

"But the whole thing is fantastic," said Marie. "What *are* you?"

"I'm a Silkie," he answered. "The *first* Silkie."

# I

NAT CEMP, a class-C Silkie, awakened in his selective fashion and perceived with those perceptors which had been asleep that he was now quite close to the spaceship whose approach he had first sensed an hour before.

Momentarily, he softened the otherwise steel-hard chitinous structure of his outer skin, so that the area became sensitive to light waves in the humanly visible spectrum. These he now recorded through a lens arrangement that utilized a portion of the chitin for distance viewing.

There was a sudden pressure in his body as it adjusted to the weakening of the barrier between it and the vacuum of space. He experienced the peculiar sensation that came whenever the stored oxygen in the chitin was used up at an excessive rate, for vision was always extremely demanding of oxygen. And then, having taken a series of visual measurements, he hardened the chitin again. Instantly, oxygen consumption returned to normal.

What he had seen with his telescopic vision upset him. It was a V ship.

Now the V's, as Cemp knew, did not normally attack a full-grown Silkie. But there had been reports recently of unusual V activity. Several Silkies had been psychologically harassed. This group might conceivably discover where he was going and use all their energy to prevent his arrival.

Even as he considered whether to avoid them or to board them—as Silkies often did—he sensed that the ship was shifting its course ever so slightly toward him. The decision was made for him. The V's wanted contact.

In terms of space orientation, the ship was neither up nor down in relation to him, of course. But he sensed the ship's own artificial gravity and adopted it as a frame of reference. By that standard its approach was somewhat below him.

As Cemp watched it with upper-range perception that registered in his brain like very sharp radar blips, the ship slowed and made a wide turn, and presently it was moving in the same direction as he but at a slightly slower speed. If he kept going as he was, he would catch up with it in a few minutes.

Cemp did not veer away. In the blackness of space ahead and below, the V ship grew large. He had measured it as being about a mile wide, half a mile thick, and three miles long.

Having no breathing apparatus, since he obtained his oxygen entirely by electrolytic interchange, Cemp could not sigh. But he felt an equivalent resignation, a sadness at the bad luck that had brought him into contact with such a large group of V's at so inopportune a time.

As he came level with it, the ship lifted gently until it was only yards away. In the darkness on the deck below, Cemp saw that several dozen V's were waiting for him. Like himself, they wore no spacesuits; for the time being, they were completely adjusted to the vacuum of space. In the near background, Cemp could see a lock that led into the interior of the ship. The outer chamber was open. Through its transparent wall he saw the water inside.

A basic longing in Cemp twinged with anticipatory pleasure. He reacted with a startled shudder, thinking in dismay, *Am I that close to the change?*

Cemp, in the C-Silkie stage entirely a creature of space, settled awkwardly on the deck. The special bone structures that had once been legs were sensitive to molecular activity within solid masses; therefore, it was through energy interchanges within the bone itself that he felt himself touch the metal.

In a sense, then, he stood there. But he balanced himself with energy flows and not with muscular contractions and expansions. There were no muscles. It was with magnetic force that he attached himself to the deck and with internal control that he moved, one after the other, the virtually solid blocks of highly differentiated bone.

He walked forward like a two-legged being, feeling the stretch of the elasticized bone of his legs. Walking was an intricate procedure for him. It meant softening the tough bone each time, then rehardening it. Although he had learned long ago how to walk, still he was slow. He who could streak through space at fifty Gs' acceleration walked on the deck of the V liner at a mile an hour and was happy that he could show a semblance of movement in such an environment.

He walked to where the V's stood, pausing a few feet from the nearest chunky figure.

At first look, a V seemed to be a slightly smaller Silkie, but Cemp knew that these bitter creatures were Variants—V for Variant. It was always difficult to determine which type of V one was looking at. The differences were internal and not readily detectable. So he had his first purpose—to establish the identity of the V's on this ship.

To communicate his message, he utilized that function of his brain which, before it was understood, had been labeled telepathy.

There was a pause, and then a V who had stood well back in the group replied, with the same communication method, "We have a reason, sir, for not identifying ourselves. And so we ask you to please bear with us until you understand our problems."

"Secrecy is illegal," Cemp replied curtly.

The answer was surprisingly free of the usual V hostility. "We are not trying to be difficult. My name is Ralden, and we want you to see something."

"What?"

"A boy, now nine years old. He's the V child of a Silkie and a breather, and he recently showed extreme variant qualities. We want permission to destroy him."

"Oh!" said Cemp. He was instantly disturbed. He had a fleeting awareness that his son, from his own first mating period, would now be nine.

Relationship, of course, didn't matter. Silkies never saw their children, and his training required him to put all Silkie offspring on the same footing. But in the uneasy peace that reigned among the ordinary humans, the Special People, and the two surviving classes of Silkies, one of the nightmares was that a high-ability V would show up someday in the unstable world of Variants.

The fear had proved unfounded. From time to time, Silkies who boarded the V ships learned that some promising boy had been executed by the V's themselves. Far from welcoming a superior child, the V's seemed to fear that if allowed to become full-grown he would be a natural leader and would threaten their freedom.

The extermination of promising boys now required the permission of a Silkie, which explained the secrecy. If they failed to obtain permission, they might still kill the youngster, trusting that the murder ship would never be identified.

"Is that the reason?" Cemp demanded.

It was.

Cemp hesitated. He sensed within himself the entire remarkable complex of sensations that meant that he was about to change. This was no time for him to spend a day or so aboard a V ship.

Yet if he didn't stay, it would be tantamount to granting permission for the execution, sight unseen. And that, he realized, could not be permitted.

"You have done well," he communicated gravely. "I shall come aboard."

The entire group of V's moved along with him to the lock, huddling together as the great steel door rolled shut behind them, closing them away from the vacuum of space. The water came in silently. Cemp could see it exploding into gas as it poured into the utter emptiness of the lock. But presently, as the narrow space filled up, it began to hold its liquid form, and it roiled and rushed around the extremities of the beings in the little group.

The feel of it was exquisitely pleasurable. Cemp's bones tried to soften automatically, and he had to fight to hold them hard. But when the water closed over the upper part of his body, Cemp let the living barrier that made up his outer skin grow soft. Because the feel of the water excited him, now that the change was so near, he had to exercise a conscious restraint. He wanted to suck the warm, delightful liquid with visible enjoyment through the gills that were now being exposed, but it seemed to him that such a display of exuberance might give away his condition to the more experienced V's.

Around him, the V's were going through the transformation from their space form to their normal gill state. The inner lock opened, and the entire group swam through with casual ease. Behind them, the inner lock door slid shut, and they were inside the ship itself or, rather, in the first of the many big tanks that made up the interior.

Cemp, using his vision now, looked around for identifying objects. But it was the usual dim watery world with transplanted sea life. Seaweed swayed in the strong currents that, Cemp knew, were kept in motion by a powerful pumping system. He could feel the surge of the water at each impulse from the pumps. As always, he began to brace himself for that surge, accepting it, letting it become one of the rhythms of his life.

## II

CEMP HAD no problems in this environment. Water was a natural element for him, and in the transformation from Silkie to human fish he had lost only a few of his Silkie abilities. The entire Silkie inner world of innumerable sensations remained. There were nerve centers that, both separately and in combination, tuned in on different energy flows. In early days, they would have been called senses. But instead of the five to which, for many centuries, human beings had limited their awareness, the Silkie could record 184 different kinds of sense impressions over a wide range of intensity.

The result was an immense amount of internal "noise" as stimulation poured incessantly in upon him. From his earliest days, control of what his sense receptors recorded had been the principal objective of his training and education.

The water flowed rhythmically through his gills as Cemp swam with the others through the watery fairyland of a warm tropical sea. As he looked ahead, he saw that the water universe was changing because of their approach. The coral was a new, creamier color. Ten thousand sea worms had withdrawn their bright heads into their tiny holes. Presently, as the group passed, they began to come out again. The coral turned orange, then purple and orange, then other shades of colors and combinations. And all this was but one tiny segment of the submarine landscape.

A dozen fish in blues and greens and purples darted up the canyon. Their wild beauty was appealing. They were an old life form, Nature-evolved, untouched by the magic of the scientific knowledge that had finally solved so many of the mysteries of life. Cemp reached with webbed fingers for a fish that darted close to him. It whirled away in a flurry of tiny water currents. Cemp grinned happily, and the warm water washed into his open mouth—so far had he softened.

He was already smaller. There had been a natural shrinkage from the tense, bony Silkie body. The newly forming muscles were contracted, and the now internalized bone structure was down to a length of seven feet from its space maximum of ten.

Of the thirty-nine V's who had come out to help persuade Cemp to board the ship, thirty-one, he learned by inquiry, were among the common variant types. The easiest state for them to be in was the fish condition in which they lived. They could be humans for brief periods, and they could be Silkies for periods that varied with these particular persons from a few hours to a week or so. All thirty-nine had some control of energy in limited amounts.

Of the remaining eight, three were capable of controlling very considerable energy, one could put up barriers to energy, and four could be breathers for extended periods of time.

They were all intelligent beings, as such things were judged. But Cemp, who could detect on one or the other of his numerous receptor systems subtle body odors and temperatures in water and out and could read meaning into the set of bone and muscle, sensed from each of these a strong emotional mixture of discontent, anger, petulance, and something even more intense—hatred. As he nearly always did with V's, Cemp swam close to the nearest. Then, using a particularly resistant magnetic force line as a carrier—it held its message undistorted for only a few feet—he superimposed the question "What's your secret?"

The V was momentarily startled. The reflex that was triggered into picking up the message was so on the ready that it modulated the answer onto a similar force line, and Cemp had the secret.

Cemp grinned at the effectiveness of his stratagem, pleased that he could now force a conversation. He communicated, "No one threatens V's individually or collectively. So why do you hate?"

"I *feel* threatened!" was the sullen reply.

"Since I know you have a wife—from your secret—do you also have children?"

"Yes."

"Work?"

"Yes."

"News, drama, TV?"

"Yes."

"Sport?"

"I watch it. I don't participate."

They were passing through an underwater jungle. Huge waving fronds, coral piled high, an octopus peering at them from the shadows of a cave, an eel darting away, and fish by the dozen. It was still the wild part of the ship, where the conditions of a tropical Earth ocean were duplicated. To Cemp, who had been nearly a month in space without a break, merely swimming here seemed like great sport indeed.

But all he said was, "Well, friend, that's all there is for anyone. A quiet, enjoyable existence is the most that life has to offer anyone. If you're envying me my police duties, don't! I'm inured to it, but I have a mating period only every nine and a half years. Would you care for that?"

The implication in his statement, that Silkies could engage in sexual activity only at intervals of nine years or so, was not true. But it was a myth that Silkies and their closest human allies, the Special People, had found it worthwhile to foster. Normal human beings particularly seemed to find great satisfaction in what they conceived to be a major defect in the otherwise enviable Silkie.

After Cemp completed his reassuring communication, the dark emotion that had been radiating from the V took on added hostility. "You're treating me like a child," he said in a grim manner. "I know something of the logic of levels. So don't give me any of these sophistries."

"It's still mostly speculation," Cemp answered gently. He added, "Don't worry, I won't tell your wife that you're unfaithful to her."

"Damn you!" said the V, and swam off.

Cemp turned to another of his companions and had a very similar discussion with him. This one's secret was that he had twice in the past year fallen asleep while on duty at one of the locks connecting the big ship with outer space.

The third person he addressed was a female. Her secret, surprisingly, was that she thought herself insane. As soon as she realized that her thought had come through to him, the substance of her communication became hysterical.

She was a graceful being, one of the breathers—but completely unnerved now. "Don't tell them!" she telepathed in terror. "They'll kill me."

Before Cemp could more than consider what an unexpected ally he had found for himself, let alone decide what made her feel she was insane, the female communicated frantically, "They're going to lure you into one of the shark tanks!" Her almost human face contorted as she realized what she had revealed.

Cemp asked quickly, "What is their overall purpose?"

"I don't know. But it's not what they said. . . . Oh, please!" She was threshing in the water now, physically disorganized. In a moment it would be noticed.

Cemp said hastily, "Don't worry—I'll help you. You have my word."

Her name, he discovered, was Mensa. She said she was very beautiful in her breather form.

Cemp had already decided that since she might be useful, he would have to let himself be drawn into the shark tank.

It was not obvious when it happened. One of the V's who was capable of energy output swam up beside him. Simultaneously but casually the others fell back.

"This way," said his guide.

Cemp followed. But it was several moments before he realized that he and his guide were on one side of a transparent wall, and the rest of the group was on the other.

He looked around for his companion. The V had dived down and was sliding into a cavern between two rock formations.

Abruptly, the water around Cemp was plunged into pitch darkness.

He grew aware that the V's were hovering beyond the transparent walls. Cemp saw movement in the swaying weeds—shadows, shapes, the glint of an eye, the play of light on a grayish body. . . . He switched to another level of perception, based on shadow pictures, and grew alert for battle.

In his fish stage, Cemp could normally fight like a superelectric eel—except that his energy discharge was a beam requiring no actual contact. The beam had the bright flash of chain lightning and was strong enough to kill a dozen sea monsters. It was formed outside his body, a confluence of two streams of oppositely charged particles.

But this was not a normal time. The change in him was too imminent. Any fight with a denizen of this sea in space would have to be with logic of levels, not with energy. He dared not waste any of his precious store of energy.

Even as he made the decision, a shark swam lazily

out of the jungle of waving fronds and just as lazily, or so it seemed, came toward him, turned on its side, and, mouth open, teeth showing, slashed at him with its enormous jaws.

Cemp impressed a pattern on an energy wave that was passing through his brain toward the beast. It was a pattern that stimulated an extremely primitive mechanism in the shark—the mechanism by which pictures were created in the brain.

The shark had no defense against controlled overstimulation of its picture-making ability. In a flash it visualized its teeth closing on its victim and imagined a bloody struggle, followed by a feast. And then, sated, stomach full, it imagined itself swimming back into the shadows, into the underwater forest in this tiny segment of a huge spaceship cruiser near Jupiter.

As the overstimulation continued, the shark's pictures ceased to connect with body movements. It drifted forward and finally bumped, unnoticing, into a coral embankment. There it hung, dreaming that it was in motion. It was being attacked through a logic related to its structure, on a level that bypassed its gigantic attack equipment.

Levels of logic. Long ago now, men had titillated themselves by opening up the older parts of the human brain where suggested pictures and sounds were as real as actual ones. It was the best level of logic, not human at all. For an animal like a shark, reality was an on-off phenomenon, a series of mechanical conditionings. Now stimulation; now none. Movement always, restless motion always—the endless need for more oxygen than was available in any one location.

Caught as it was in a suggested world of fantasy, the motionless shark body grew numb from insufficient oxygen and began to lose consciousness. Before it could really do so, Cemp communicated to the watchers, "Do you want me to kill this game fish?"

Silently, the beings beyond the transparent wall indicated where he could escape from the shark tank.

Cemp gave the monster control of itself again. But he knew it would be twenty or more minutes before the shock could wear off.

As he emerged from the shark tank a few minutes later and rejoined the V's, Cemp realized at once that their mood had changed. They were derisive of him. It was puzzling that they had adopted this attitude, for as far as they knew they were completely at his mercy.

Someone in this group must know Cemp's true condition. So . . .

He saw that they were now in a tank of water so deep that the bottom was not visible. Small schools of brightly colored fish skittered by in the green depths, and the water seemed slightly colder, more bracing; still delightful but no longer tropical. Cemp swam over to one of the V's who was capable of putting out energy. As before, he asked, "What's your secret?"

The male V's name was Gell, and his secret was that he had several times used his energy to kill rivals for the favors of certain females. He was instantly terrified that his murders would be found out. But he had no information except that the administrative officer of the ship, Riber, had sent them to meet Cemp. The name was important information.

But even more vital was Cemp's disturbing intuition that this task of duty on which he was embarked was much more important than the evidence had so far established. He divined that the shark attack was a test. But a test for what?

# III

AHEAD, SUDDENLY, Cemp could see the city.

The water at this point was crystal clear. Here were none of those millions of impurities which so often rendered the oceans of Earth murky. Through that liquid, almost as transparent as glass, the city spread before him.

Domed buildings, duplicates of the domed undersea cities on Earth, where water pressure made the shape necessary. Here, with only artificial gravity, water was held by the metal walls and had only what weight the ship's officers elected to give it. Buildings could be any reasonable size, delicately molded and even misshapen. They could be beautiful for their own sake and were not limited to the sometimes severe beauty of utility.

The building to which Cemp was taken was a soaring dome with minarets. He was guided to a lock, where only two of the breathers, Mensa and a male named Grig, stayed with him.

The water level began to drop, and air hissed in. Cemp transformed quickly into his human shape and stepped out of the airlock into the corridor of a modern airconditioned building. All three were in the nude.

The man said to the woman, "Take him to your apartment. Give him the clothes. As soon as I call, bring him to Apartment One upstairs."

Grig was walking off, when Cemp stopped him. "Where did you get that information?" he demanded.

The V hesitated, visibly frightened at being challenged by a Silkie. The expression on his face changed, and he seemed to be listening.

Instantly, Cemp activated the waking centers of a portion of his sensory equipment that he had let sleep

and waited for a response on one or more "channels."
Much as a man who smells a strong odor of sulphur
wrinkles his nose or as someone who touches a red-hot
object jerks involuntarily away, he expected a sensation
from one of the numerous senses that were now ready.
He got nothing.

It was true that in his human state, he was not so
sensitive as when he was in the Silkie state. But such a
totally negative result was outside his experience.

Grig said, "He says . . . as soon as you're dressed . . .
come."

"Who says?"

Grig was surprised. "The boy," he replied. His manner
indicated: Who else?

As he dried himself and put on the clothes Mensa
handed him, Cemp found himself wondering why she
believed herself insane. He asked cautiously, "Why do
V's have a poor opinion of themselves?"

"Because there's something better—Silkies." Her tone
was angry, but there were tears of frustration in her eyes.
She went on wearily, "I can't explain it, but I've felt
shattered ever since I was a child. Right now I have an
irrational hope that you will want to take me over and
possess me. I want to be your slave."

Though her jet-black hair was still matted and wet, it
was obvious that she had told the truth about her appearance. Her skin was creamy white, her body slim,
with graceful curves. As a breather, she was beautiful.

Cemp had no alternative. Within the next hour, he
might need what help she could give. He said quietly,
"I accept you as my slave."

Her response was violent. In a single convulsion of
movement, she ran over to him, writhing out of her
upper garments until they draped low on her hips.
"Take me!" she said urgently. "Take me as a woman!"

Cemp, who was married to a young woman of the
Special People, released himself. "Slaves don't demand,"

he said in a firm tone. "Slaves are used at the will of their masters. And my first demand as your master is, open your mind to me."

The woman drew away from him, trembling. "I can't," she said. "The boy forbids it."

Cemp asked, "What in you makes you feel insane?"

She shook her head. "Something . . . connected with the boy," she said. "I don't know what."

"Then you're his slave, not mine," said Cemp coldly.

Her eyes begged him. "Free me!" she whispered. "I can't do it myself."

"Where's Apartment One?" Cemp asked.

She told him, "You can take the stairway or the elevator."

Cemp went by the stairway. He needed a few minutes, just a few, to determine his course of action. He decided . . .

See the boy! Determine his fate. Talk to Riber, the administrative officer of the ship. Punish Riber! Order this ship to a check-in point!

These decisions were hardened in his mind as he reached the upper level and pressed the button beside the door of Apartment One.

The door swung open noiselessly. Cemp walked in—and there was the boy.

He was slightly under five feet tall, as fine-looking a human child as Cemp had ever seen. The youngster was watching a TV screen set into one wall of the big room. When Cemp entered the boy turned lazily and said, "I was interested in seeing what you would do with that shark, in view of your condition."

*He knew!*

The realization hit Cemp hard. He braced himself and agreed within himself to die, to make no bargains to avoid exposure, to come to his final decision with even greater care.

The boy said, "You couldn't possibly do anything else."

Cemp was recovering, and now he was curious. He had set up a complete no-signal condition within himself. Yet the boy was reading detailed signals. How was he doing it?

Smiling faintly, the boy shook his head.

Cemp said, "If you dare not tell, it isn't much of a method. I deduce that if I can find it out, I can defeat it."

The boy laughed, made a gesture of dismissal, and changed the subject. "Do you believe I should be killed?"

Cemp looked into the bright gray eyes that regarded him with a boyish mischievousness and felt a qualm. He was being played with by someone who regarded himself as untouchable. The question was, was the boy fooling himself or was it real?

"It's real," said the youngster.

And if it was real—Cemp's analysis continued—were there built-in restraining factors such as kept Silkies under control?

The boy said curtly, "That I will not answer."

"Very well," Cemp turned away. "If you persist in that decision, then my judgment is that you are outside the law. No person who cannot be controlled will ever be permitted to live in the solar system. But I'm going to give you a little while in which to change your mind. My advice is that you decide to be a law-abiding citizen."

He turned and left the apartment. And the important reality was that he was allowed to do so.

## IV

GRIG WAS waiting in the hallway outside. He seemed eager to please. Cemp, who wanted to meet Riber, asked if Riber was a breather. Riber was not; so Cemp and Grig took to the water.

Cemp was guided to an enormous depth, to where several domes were fixed to the inner hull of the ship. There, in a water-filled labyrinth of metal and plastic, he found Riber. The administrative leader of the ship turned out to be a long, strong fish being with the peculiar protruding eyes of the fish state. He was floating beside a message-receiving machine. In one hand he held the transmitter for the machine. He looked at Cemp and turned the machine on.

He said aloud in the underwater language, "I think our conversation should be recorded. I don't think I can trust a Silkie to make a fair report on this special situation."

Cemp acquiesced without argument. The interchange began with Riber making what seemed to be a completely frank statement. He said, "This ship and all aboard are controlled by that remarkable boy. He is not always here, and so for the most part we do as we always have. But those people who went out to meet you had no way of resisting his commands. If you can deal with him, then obviously we shall be free again. But if you can't, then we are his servants, like it or not."

Cemp said, "There has to be some vulnerable level. Why, for example, do you do as he wants?"

Riber said, "I laughed when he first told me what he wanted. But when I came to, hours later, I realized that I had done everything he desired while I was unconscious. As a result, I now do it consciously. This has been going on for about a year, Earth time."

Cemp questioned Riber closely. That he had continued physical functioning when he was under the boy's control indicated that the boy's principal method of inducing unconsciousness was to shut off normal perception.

Considering that, Cemp remembered the V whose secret was that he had fallen asleep while tending one of the outer locks. At Cemp's request, lock attendants were assembled. He interviewed each one privately with the question "What's your secret?"

Seven of the twenty revealed, in this unwitting fashion, that they had slept while on duty. It turned out to be that simple. The boy had arrived at the lock entrance, blanked out the mind of the attendant, and entered the ship.

It seemed to Cemp that he need examine no further. There was a frame of logic. The problem, which for a time had seemed to involve some new and intricate kind of telekinetic control, was beginning to look much more mundane.

He returned to the woman's apartment and put on clothes again. Mensa went with him to the door. She whispered, "Don't you dare leave this ship without making love to me. I need to feel that I belong to you."

Basically, that was not so, Cemp knew. She lived by reversals. She would always want what she did not have, despise or reject what she had. But he reassured her that he meant well by her, and then he went up again to Apartment One.

It seemed to Cemp as he walked in that the boy's face was flushed and that the eyes that had been so bright were duller. Cemp said softly, "If I can figure it out, so can any Silkie. You went to a lot of trouble. Which tells me that you do have limitations."

Silkies could approach a vessel undetected, if they

were prepared to manipulate energy waves. But the method was involved, requiring training.

Cemp said, "Well, you know my thoughts. Which one is correct?"

Silence.

"Your problem," said Cemp emphatically, "is that the Special People take no chances with dangerous deviates."

He hoped the boy understood how ultimately determined the Special People were.

Abruptly, the boy sighed. "I might as well admit it. I am Tem, your son. When I realized it was you approaching the ship, I thought I'd have a look at my father. The truth is, I became frightened that those abilities which you found so unusual would be detected. So I've been out here in space setting up an operating base to which I could retreat for my own protection. But I realize I need help, I think some changes should be made in our relationship with human beings. Other than that, I'm willing to conform and be reeducated."

For Cemp, it was the decisive clarification. Then and there he made up his mind—there would be no execution.

Hastily—for Cemp was a man in a hurry—they discussed the situation. Cemp would have to tell of this meeting when he got back to Earth. There was no way by which a Silkie could conceal the facts from the perceptive Special People. And for many months, while he was in his mating stage, he would have no control of energy. During that period the boy would be at the mercy of a highly prejudiced law.

Tem was disdainful. "Don't worry about me. I'm ready for them."

It was rebel talk, dangerous and unfortunate. But this was not the moment to point that out. Such matters could be left until they got home.

"You'd better start now," said the boy, "but as you'll see, I'll get to Earth before you do."

Cemp did not pause to find out how he would achieve this miracle of speed. That, too, would have to wait.

As Cemp removed his clothes in Mensa's apartment, he said to her with considerable pride, "The boy is my son."

Her eyes widened. "Your son!" she said. "But—" she broke off.

"What's the matter?" Cemp asked.

"Nothing." She spoke mechanically. "I was surprised, that's all."

Cemp finished dressing, then went over to her and kissed her lightly on the forehead. He said, "I sense that you are involved in a love relationship."

She shook her head. "Not now. Not since . . ." She paused. She seemed bewildered.

It was no time to check on a woman's love life. If ever a man was in a hurry, he was.

When Cemp had left Mensa's apartment, the boy came in. "You almost gave me away," he said in a tone that was wholly unchildlike.

She cringed. "I'm only a V," she pleaded.

He began to change, to grow. Presently, a fully adult human male stood before her. He directed toward her an energy wave that must have exerted an enormous attraction to her, for in spite of the deepening expression of distaste on her face, she swayed toward him. When she was within a foot of him, he cut off the wave. She drew back immediately.

The man laughed. But he turned away from her, and for a few moments, then, he opened a communication line to someone on a planet of a distant star.

He said in a silent interchange, "I have finally risked confrontation with a Silkie, one of the powerful inhabitants of this system. He is guided by an idea called levels of logic. I discovered that his had to do with his only offspring, a boy he had never seen. I distorted his interest in this child in a subtle way. I think I can now land safely on the principal planet, which is called Earth."

"To distort it, you must have had to use him as a channel."

"Yes. It was the one risk I took with him."

"What about the other channels you have used, Di-isarinn?"

The man glanced at Mensa. "With one possible exception, they would resist any attempt of a Silkie to explore their minds. They're a rebel group called V's and are suspicious of, and hostile to, the other people in the system. The exception is a V woman who is completely under my control."

"Why not annihilate her?"

"These people have some kind of a sensitive telepathetic connection, which they seem to be able to manipulate but which I have not wholly solved. If she died I think the others would know instantly. Therefore, I cannot do what I normally would."

"What about the Silkie?"

"He's heading to Earth in a state of delusion. Equally important, he is due to suffer a physiological change that will strip him of all his present offensive and defensive powers. I intend to let this physical process run its course—and then kill him."

# V

CEMP HAD relayed the story through Satellite Five-R to his contact, Charley Baxter, at the Silkie Authority. When he reached the satellite and changed to human form, he found a radiogram from Charley waiting for him. It said;

HAVE PICKED UP BOY. AUTHORITY FORBIDS YOU TO LAND UNTIL THIS IS ALL SETTLED.

*Till you've done away with him, you mean!* Cemp thought angrily. the official action surprised him. It was an unexpected obstacle.

The commander of the satellite, a normal intelligent human being, who had handed him the message, said, "Mr. Cemp, I have received instructions not to let you on any ferry to Earth until further notice. This is very unusual."

"Unusual" was an understatement. Silkies ordinarily moved freely to and from Earth.

Cemp made up his mind. "I'm going out into space again," he said in a matter-of-fact tone.

"Aren't you due for a change?" The officer seemed doubtful about letting him go.

Cemp smiled wryly and told the Silkie joke about such things, how Silkies were like some mothers-to-be who kept having false labor pains. Off to the hospital they went, lay there in bed, at last returned home. And so, after several false alarms, baby was finally born in a taxicab.

"Well, sir," said the man unhappily, "you do as you please. But there aren't any taxicabs in space."

"It's not that instantaneous; you can fight it off for hours," said Cemp, who had been fighting it off for hours. Before he left, Cemp sent a radiogram to his wife.

DEAR JOANNE: DELAYED BY DISPUTE. WILL ADVISE WHEN TO MEET. BUT SOON. CALL CHARLEY. HE'LL FILL YOU IN. ALL MY LOVE, NAT.

The coded message would upset her, he knew. But he did not doubt that she would meet him at their pre-arranged rendezvous, as he wanted. She would come, if only to find out on behalf of the Special People what he was up to.

Once out in space, Cemp headed for a point over the South Pole, and then he began his entry.

He came in fast. According to theory, that was the only way an unprotected approach should be made. The poles were relatively free of radiation. There, where the magnetic field of the planetary body was bent inward right down to the ground, the potent Van Allen radiation belt was a minimum threat.

Nonetheless, there were two periods of severe bombardment, one of high-energy stripped nuclei, the other of X rays. The X rays did him no harm, and for the most part the stripped nuclei passed right through his body as if it were a hard vacuum. Those nuclei which hit, however, left a small wake of radioactivity. Hastily, Cemp expelled the more seriously damaged cells, with that special ability Silkies had of eliminating damaged parts of their bodies.

As he entered the atmosphere, Cemp gradually activated the planet's magnetic force lines behind him. Even as they began to glow brightly, he felt the radar beams bouncing off him from below. But they were not a problem now. Radar would register the movement of his body and the pyrotechnic display to his rear as one phenomenon. The outward appearance was of a meteorite shooting toward the ground.

His entrance being slantwise in the same direction as Earth's rotation, his speed of entry was such that he could easily absorb, or radiate from him, the heat of his passage through the air. At ten miles up, he slowed even more and came down in the sea north of Antarctica about a thousand miles from the lower tip of South America. The cold waters quickly washed from his Silkie body the radioactive debris that still clung to the outer bone. He darted along about five hundred feet up, using the water as a coolant by slowing and diving into it whenever he got too hot. It was a fine balancing of extremely rapid acceleration and deceleration, but he made it to near where he lived at the lower tip of Florida in slightly more than forty minutes, the last five of which were wholly underwater.

As he surfaced within sight of the beach, he transformed to his fish stage and then, two hundred feet from shore, to human. He had already seen Joanne's car parked on the road behind a sand dune. He did the overhand crawl to get to shallow water and ran against the surging waves up the embankment to where she lay on a blanket, watching him.

She stood up, a slender, very pretty woman, blonde and blue eyed. Her classically even features were white and set now as she handed him a towel. Cemp dried himself and climbed into the clothes she had brought. A few minutes later they were in the car, and at this point she accepted his kiss. But she still withheld her thoughts, and her body was rigid with disapproval.

When she finally communicated, it was verbally and not by direct energy. "Do you realize," she said, "that if you persist in this you will be the first Silkie in over a hundred years to get himself punished or executed?"

That she spoke out loud confirmed Cemp's suspicion. He was now certain that she had reported his illegal entry to the Silkie Authority and that people were listening in to this conversation. He felt no blame of Joanne. He even surmised that all the Special People were prepared to help him through this trying period. They were probably also speeding up the investigation of Tem, so that the execution would be quickly over with.

"What are you going to do, Nat?" She sounded anxious now, rather than angry. There was color in her face for the first time.

At some depth within, Cemp felt vaguely surprised at how determined he was. But the awareness did not trigger any question in him. He said coolly, "If they kill that boy, I'll know the reason why."

She said softly, "I never realized that a Silkie could have so much feeling for his child, whom he has not seen since birth. After all, I too had to give him up. My deconditioning took."

Cemp was irritated. "It's not personal," he said curtly.

She said with sudden emotion, "Then you know the reason very well. This boy evidently has a method of concealing his thoughts and of reading minds—according to your own account—that even you could not penetrate. With such a person, the Special People will not have their historic protection. It becomes a matter of policy."

"In making my report," said Cemp, "I advised a five-year study and reeducation program for the boy. That's the way it's going to be."

She seemed not to hear. As if thinking out loud, she said, "Silkies were mutated by humans, on the basis of the great biological discoveries of the last half of the twentieth century. When the basic chemical unit of life, DNP, was isolated, major advances in life forms, other than those naturally spawned in Nature, became possible. Because the first transformations were to the fish stage, the new beings were called Silkies, after an old song.

"But it had to be done carefully. The Silkie could not be permitted to breed as he pleased. So his genes, which endow him with so many marvelous senses and abilities, also contain certain limitations. He can be a man, a fish, a Silkie at will. So long as he does it by body control, he has nearly all his Silkie abilities in any of these forms. But every nine and a half years he has to become a human being again, in order to mate. It's built into him, where he can't interfere with it.

"Silkies who long ago tried to eliminate this phase of the cycle were executed. At the time of such a compulsive change to human form, he loses all his Silkie abilities and becomes fallibly human. That's the great hold we have over him. Then we can punish him for anything illegal he did as a Silkie. Another hold is that there are no female Silkies. If the issue of a Silkie mating with a woman of the Special People is a girl, she is not a Silkie. That, too, is built into his genes—"

She broke off, then went on, "The Special People are a tiny, tiny portion of the main human stream who, it was discovered, had a spontaneous ability to read the minds of Silkies. They used this to establish administrative ascendancy while there were still only a few Silkies, and thus they protected themselves and the human race from beings who would otherwise have overwhelmed them."

She finished in a puzzled tone, "You've always agreed that such protection was necessary, for human beings to survive. Have you changed your mind?" When Cemp did not reply, she urged, "Why don't you go to the Silkie Authority and talk to Charley Baxter? A single conversation with him will get you further than any rebellion." She added quickly, "Tem is there. So you'll have to go there anyway. Please, Nat."

It wasn't so much, then, that Cemp agreed with what she said—he thought of her suggestion very distinctly as offering a way to get inside the building. But he was not too surprised as his helijet came down on the roof at Silkie Authority to see Charley Baxter waiting for him, tall, rather good-looking, thin, unusually pale.

As they rode down in an elevator, Cemp felt himself pass through an energy screen that instantly sealed off the pulsations from the outside world. And that was normal enough except for the force that was driving the screen. He sensed that the power backing it was enormous enough to protect a city, or even a substantial part of the planet.

Cemp glanced questioningly at Baxter and met a pair of sober, serious eyes. The man said quietly, "At this point, you may read me."

What he read in Baxter's mind was that his own radiogram about Tem had caused a hasty examination of Tem's record. As a result, they had decided that the boy was normal and that something very serious had happened to Cemp.

"At no time," said Baxter, "has your son been in danger. Now, take a look at that TV picture. Which one is Tem? One is."

They had walked from the elevator into a large room. On the TV screen on one wall was a street scene. Several boys were approaching what must have been a hidden camera, for they showed no awareness of its presence.

Cemp's gaze flicked across the strange faces. "Never saw any of them before," he said.

"The boy to your right is your son," said Baxter.

Cemp looked, then turned and stared at Baxter. And because his brain had energy relationships that bypassed mere neuron connections, he got the whole picture in a single flash of understanding. That instantaneous comprehension included analytical awareness of how his duty to protect all Silkie children had been skillfully twisted by his pseudo-son. It leaped on to a lightning examination of the energy level that had signaled him.

Almost immediately, he realized that the signal was the only direct contact that had been made by the boy on the V ship. In every other way, the fraudulent Tem had merely been a recipient of signals.

He grew conscious of Baxter's bright eyes watching him. The man asked breathlessly, "Think we can do anything?"

It was too soon to answer that. Cemp was gratefully realizing how he had been protected by the Special People. It seemed to him that if he had suspected the truth at any moment before being taken behind the energy screen that now guarded him—the false Tem would probably have tried to annihilate him.

Baxter was speaking again. "You sit down here, and let's see what the computer makes of the one signal you received."

The computer extrapolated three structural frames that might fit the false Tem. Cemp and Baxter studied the coded messages with amazement, for they had not actually considered anything beyond an unusual V frame.

All three formulated structures were alien. A quick analysis established that two of the three did not require secrecy on the part of so powerful a being as the invader undoubtedly was. Therefore, the third frame, involving a gruesome form of esoteric sex climaxed by the ritual murder of one partner by the other, like spiders, was the most likely.

Baxter's voice had in it the desire not to believe. "That picture of their needing a lot of love objects—could that be real?" He finished in a subdued tone, "I'll alert all Silkies, mobilize our other forces—but can you do anything at once?"

Cemp, who had already adjusted his sensory system to include all three alien frames, was tense and afraid. He said, "I ask myself where he would go, and of course, it would be to my home. Do you think Joanne would have got there yet? Was she supposed to head some-where else?"

He saw that Baxter was shaking his head. . . .

Cemp hurried through a door that led to a wide balcony, transformed to Silkie, and did a partial cut-off of gravity combined with control of magnetic force lines . . . a man in a far greater hurry than he had ever been in before.

# VI

He ENTERED the large house by the sea in his human form, the better to run the last few yards and maneuver in corridors. And because he had adjusted to the alien sensory structure, his arrival was only partially signaled.

He found Joanne in the master bedroom, half-undressed.

She had never seemed more attractive. Her smile, warm and inviting and friendly, drew him. She was in some state of excitement that communicated itself to him, stirring an impulse so basic that it was as if a fine, translucent sheath dropped over his senses, blurring his view of reality. The woman, almost luminescent in a fleshly radiance, lay on the pink bed, and his whole being focused on her. For a long moment, nothing else existed. They were two people intensely in love.

Breathless, astounded by that hideous instant power, Cemp put his thought on the possible fate of the real Joanne, put his attention on fear for her—and broke the spell.

The rage, hate, and violence that had been building up in him broke through.

But the magnetically controlled radiation that Cemp launched at the creature crackled harmlessly against a magnetically controlled energy screen. Frothing, he plunged at the being, grabbed at him with his bare hands.

For seconds they grappled, the almost nude woman and the wholly naked Cemp. Then Cemp was flung back by muscles that were ten times stronger than his own.

He bounded to his feet, but he was sobered, thinking

again. He began to consider the entire problem of Earth in relation to this creature and the threat it represented.

The duplicate of Joanne was changing. The body in front of him became that of a man with the frilly clothes of a woman's underdress still draped around his hips, but there was nothing feminine in his manner. Eyes blazing with the infinite violence potential of the male, the entity locked gazes with Cemp.

Cemp was feeling a desperate anxiety about his wife, but it did not even occur to him to ask this creature about her. He said, instead, "I want you to leave. We'll communicate with you when you're a million miles out in space."

The handsome human face of the other broke into a disdainful smile. "I'll go. But I sense in you a plan to learn from me where I come from. That will never happen."

Cemp replied in a level tone, "We'll see what two thousand Silkies can get out of you."

The being's skin glistened with health, shone with confidence and power. He said, "Perhaps I should inform you that we Kibmadine have achieved a total control of all the forces that Silkies control only partially."

Cemp said, "Many rigidities can envelop one flexibility."

The other said in an uncompromising voice, "Don't attack me. The price would be too high."

He started to turn away. And there was a moment, then, when Cemp had another thought, another feeling —a reluctance to let this being go without some attempt to reach across the abyss that separated them. Because this was man's first contact with an alien intelligence. For a few fleeting seconds, Cemp remembered the thousand dreams that human beings had had of such a meeting. But then his hesitation came to its inevitable end as the infinitely hostile reality moved in to fill the endless void between them.

Instants later, the alien was out on the path, dissolving, changing—and gone.

Cemp contacted Baxter and said, "Line me up with another Silkie so that he can take over. I'm really awfully close to my change."

He was lined up through the Silkie communications hub with a Silkie named Jedd. Meanwhile, Baxter said, "I'm on my way over. I have been given a lot of governmental power."

Cemp found Joanne in one of the spare bedrooms. She lay on the bed, fully dressed, breathing slowly and deeply. He sent a quick flow of energy through her brain. The reflexes that were stirred reassured him that she was merely sleeping. He also picked up some of the alien energy that was still in her cells. The information superimposed on this energy told a story that made it instantly obvious why she was still alive: The Kibmadine had used her living body as a model for his duplication of her.

On this occasion, at least, the creature had been after bigger game—a Silkie.

Cemp did not try to rouse the sleeping woman, but he was greatly relieved as he went out into the patio, which overlooked a white, sandy beach and the timeless blue ocean beyond. He sat there until presently Baxter joined him.

They had already communicated mentally, and now Baxter said, "I sense a doubt in you."

Cemp nodded.

Baxter asked gently, "What do you fear?"

"*Death!*"

It was a feeling deep inside him.

Sitting there, he made up his mind, for the second time since he had become involved with the alien, to die if necessary. And with that decision, he began to turn on all his receptors, after first carefully tuning out local Earth noise. TV, radio, radar, innumerable energies from machines—these had to be shut away from him. Swiftly, then, he began to "hear" the signals from throughout space.

Long before Silkies it had been known that space was alive with messages; the entire sidereal universe pulsed with an incredible number of vibrations. Hour on hour and year by year, Silkies lived with that ceaseless "noise," and most of their early training was entirely directed to the development of selective sleep and rest and wakefulness mechanisms for each receptor.

Now, those which were asleep awakened; those which were at rest, became alert.

His brain came to peak awareness, and he began to sense the near stars, the distant stars, the clusters, the galaxies. Every star had its own complex signal. Nowhere was there a duplication or even a close similarity.

The universe that he tuned in upon was composed entirely of individuals. Cemp appraised the distance of each star, the uniqueness of each signal. Friendly space world! Every star being exactly and precisely what it was and where it was gave meaning to the immense stellar universe. There was no chaos. He experienced his own location in space and time, and it gave him a certainty of the basic rightness of things.

# VII

CEMP'S PROBING awareness came back from its far-flung ranging to a spot about a million miles from Earth. There he paused to let the signals come in from all the space between that point and Earth.

Without opening his eyes, he said to Baxter, "I don't read him. He must have gone around the planet and put the mass of Earth between us. Are the reflectors ready?"

Baxter spoke over a phone line that had been kept open for him. Previously alerted Telstar and astronomical satellites were placed at Cemp's disposition. Through one of the reflectors, he focused on the invading entity.

Cemp said to the alien, "Above everything else, we want information."

The alien said, "Perhaps I should tell you our history."

And so Cemp was given the story of the eternal lovers, more than a million beings who moved from one planetary system to another, each time altering themselves to the form of the inhabitants and establishing a love relationship with them. But it was a love relationship that meant pain and death for their love objects. Only twice had the lovers met beings of sufficient power to repel them. In each case, the Kibmadine had destroyed the entire system.

Di-isarinn finished, "No additional information is available to you."

Cemp broke contact. A shaken Baxter said, "Do you think that was true information?"

Cemp answered that he thought it was. He finished with finality, "Our job is to find out one thing—where does he come from?—and then destroy him."

46

"But how do you propose to do this?"

It was a good question. His single clash with the creature had brought him up hard against a wall of incredible power.

Cemp sank lower into his settee and with closed eyes considered the problem of a race of beings who had complete control of body change. Many times in those long duty watches out in space, he had pondered such possibilities; for the cell could grow and ungrow, divide, split off, fall away, and re-form, all within a few seconds. In the twilight zone of life where the virus, the bacteriums, and the cell had their complex being, the enormous speed of change had made possible the almost instantaneous orderly altering of human to Silkie and back again.

The invader could apparently change to an infinite number of forms with equal rapidity, assuming any body shape at will.

But the logic of levels applied to the Kibmadine's every action.

From somewhere behind Cemp, Baxter said, "Are you sure?" His voice sounded incredulous.

Cemp had two reactions to the question—extreme joy at the hope that his analysis brought . . . and a stronger conviction. He said aloud, "Yes, logic applies. But for him we'll need the closest contact of the energies involved. Inches would be better than feet, feet better than yards. So I'll have to go out there in person."

"Out where?" Baxter asked. He sounded astounded.

"To his ship."

"Do you think he has a ship?"

"Of course he has one. Anything else would be impractical for his operations."

Cemp was patient as he made his explanation. He had observed that even the Special People had exaggerated ideas on such matters. They tended to accept that Silkies were much more capable than they really were. But the logic of it was simple—coming in toward a sun, one could utilize its full gravitational pull to get up speed. Right now the Kibmadine would be "climbing the ladder" of the planets, cutting off the sun's gravity from behind, opening up to the pull of Jupiter and the outer planets.

No sensible being would try to bridge the distances between stars by such a method. So there was a ship. There had to be.

Cemp said, "Order a spaceship for me, complete with a tank of water that can be moved."

"You expect to change before you get there?"

"It'll happen any minute."

Amazed, Baxter said, "You intend to confront the most powerful being that we can imagine without a single bit of energy of your own available?"

"Yes," said Cemp. "It's the only way we'll get him within inches of the energy source I want installed in the tank. For heaven's sake, man, get started."

Reluctantly, Baxter reached for the phone.

# VIII

As CEMP had expected, he began his change en route. By the time he was put aboard the Kibmadine ship he was already in a tank of water in his first compulsive change, which was to the fish state.

He would be a class-B Silkie for slightly more than two months.

As Di-isarinn came finally to the tiny ship in its remote orbit beyond Pluto, he noticed at once that the entrance mechanism had been tampered with, and he sensed the Cemp's presence aboard.

In the course of countless millenia, Di-isarinn's reflexes had fallen into disuse, so he had no anxiety. But he did recognize that here were all the appearances of a trap.

In a flash, he checked to ensure that there was no source of energy aboard that could destroy him. There was none—no relay; nothing.

A faint energy emanated from the tank, but it had no purpose that Di-isarinn could detect.

He wondered scathingly if these human beings somehow expected to work a bluff whereby he would be impelled by uncertainty to stay away from his own ship.

With that thought, he activated the entrance mechanism, entered, transformed to human form, walked over to the tank that stood in the center of the tiny cabin, and looked down at Cemp, who lay at the bottom.

Di-isarinn said, "If it's a bluff, I couldn't possibly yield to it because I have nowhere else to go."

In his fish state, Cemp could hear and understand human words, but he could not speak them.

Di-isarinn persisted. "It's interesting that the one

Silkie whom I now cannot read has taken the enormous risk of coming aboard. Your computer helped you to adjust to me, but perhaps you were more affected by the desire I attempted to arouse in your home than appeared at the time. Perhaps you long for the ecstasy and the anguish that I offered."

Cemp was thinking tensely, *It's working. He doesn't notice how he got onto that subject.*

The logic of levels was beginning to take effect. It was a strange world, the world of logic. For nearly all his long history, man had been moved by unsuspected mechanisms in his brain and his nervous system. A sleep center put him to sleep, a waking center woke him up, a rage mechanism mobilized him for attack, a fear complex propelled him in flight. There were a hundred or more other mechanisms, each with its special task, each in itself a marvel of perfect functioning but degraded by man's uncomprehending obedience to a chance triggering of one or another.

During this period, all civilization consisted of codes of honor and conduct and of attempts noble and ignoble to rationalize the simplicities underneath. Finally came a developing comprehension and control of the neural mechanisms—one, then another, then many.

The real Age of Reason began. On the basis of that reason Cemp asked himself, was the Kibmadine level lower or higher than, for example, that of the shark? It was lower, he decided. The comparison would be, if man had brought cannibalism into civilization with him. A lower level of logic applied to that.

The shark was relatively pure within his frame. He lived by the feedback system and managed a well-balanced existence. He did not age, as humans did. He grew older—and longer. It was a savagely simple system. Keep in motion; that was the law of it. What poetry that motion was, in the wide, deep sea that had spawned him! But the motion was—feel need of oxygen, get excited, swim faster; enough oxygen, slow, cruise, even stop. But not for long. Continual movement—that was the life of the shark.

Eating, of itself, was lower, more basic, went farther back into the antiquity of the cell. And so the mighty Kibmadine had brought into their innumerable forms one pattern that was vulnerable, one they wouldn't give up, no matter how much they controlled the other basic mechanisms of their bodies. . . .

Di-isarinn felt himself calm and in control. It was unfortunate that the Silkie had analyzed the Kibmadine structure so accurately. But it didn't matter. Under other circumstances, Earth might have been a planet to be destroyed. But there was no chance at all of enough Silkies being produced in time to save the system from being conquered.

And so another race would, one at a time, experience the ecstasy of being eaten as the culmination of the act of love.

What a joy it was to receive from tens of millions of cells, first resistance, terror, shrinking, and then the inversion, every part of the being craving to be eaten, longing, begging, demanding. . . .

Di-isarinn's calmness yielded to excitement as the pictures and the feelings re-formed in his mind from ten thousand remembered feasts of love objects.

*I really loved them all*, he thought sadly. It was too bad they had not been brought up to appreciate in advance the ultimate delight of the all-consuming end of the sex orgy.

It had always bothered Di-isarinn that the preliminaries had to be secret, particularly with beings who had the ability to transmit thoughts to others of their kind and thus warn them. The greatest pleasure always came when the ending was known, when part of the love play consisted in reassuring the troubled, trembling being and quieting the pounding heart.

"Someday," he had told thousands of love partners, "I shall meet someone who will eat me. And when that happens . . ."

Always he had tried to persuade them that he would rejoice as he was being devoured.

The inversion involved was a phenomenon of the life condition; the urge to succumb could be as powerful as the urge to survive.

Standing there in front of the tank, looking down at Cemp, Di-isarinn felt a quickening of emotion as the conjuration of being eaten flitted like a fantasy through his brain. He had had such pictures before, but never had they been so strong.

He did not notice that he had passed the point of no return. Without thinking, he turned away from the tank. Cemp forgotten, he transformed quickly into a remembered form, long-necked, with smooth, dappled skin and powerful teeth. He remembered the form well and lovingly. The members of the race had been love objects for the Kibmadine not long before. Their bodies had a particularly excruciating pleasure-nerve system.

Di-isarinn could scarcely wait.

Even as he became the form, his long neck twisted. A moment later, the teeth, impelled by the merciless Kibmadine biting drive, cut off an entire thigh.

The pain was so hideous that he screamed. But in his enchanted brain the scream was only an echo of the countless screams that his bite had evoked in the past. Now, as then, the sound excited him almost beyond endurance.

He bit deeper, champed harder, ate faster.

He devoured nearly one half of his own body before the imminence of death brought a baby fear from his own true past. Whimpering, blindly longing for home, he opened a line to his contact on the planet of the far sun where his kind now dwelt.

At that instant an outside force surged past him and

overwhelmed his personal communications. As one, a dozen Silkies loaded an electric charge on that line, all they believed that it could carry.

The charge that struck the distant Kibmadine totaled more than 140,000 amperes of electricity at more than 80,000 volts. It was so powerful that it smashed all the reflex defenses of Di-isarinn's fellow being and burned him in a single puff of flame and smoke.

As quickly as it had opened, the line ceased to exist. The Sol system was now only a remote, anonymous star. . . .

The tank with Cemp in it was carried to the ocean. He crawled out into the sea and breasted the incoming tide, and the fresh, bubbling liquid poured through his gills. As he reached the deep water, he submerged. Soon the thunder of the surf was behind him. Ahead were a blue sea and the great underwater shelf where a colony of class-B Silkies lived their fishlike existence.

He would dwell in their domed cities with them . . . for a time.

## IX

CEMP'S PERIOD of life as less than a class-C Silkie passed uneventfully.

Almost a year later, Nat Cemp, walking along the street, passed the man—and stopped.

Something about the other triggered a signal in that portion of his nervous system which, even in his human state, retained a portion of his Silkie ability. He couldn't remember, hard as he tried, ever having felt that particular signal before.

Cemp turned in the street and looked back. The stranger had paused at the near corner. Then, as the light became green, he walked briskly toward the far sidewalk. He was about Cemp's height of slightly over six feet and seemed about the same build—about a hundred and ninety pounds.

His hair was dark brown, like Cemp's, and he wore a dark gray suit, as did Cemp. Now that they were several hundred feet apart, the initial impression he had had of somebody familiar was not so clear.

Yet after only a slight hesitation, Cemp rapidly walked after the man, presently came up to him, and said courteously, "May I speak to you?"

The man stopped. At close range, the resemblance between them was truly remarkable, suggesting consanguinity. Blue-gray eyes, straight nose, firm mouth, strong neck, shape of ears, and the very way they held themselves were similar.

Cemp said, "I wonder if you are aware that you and I are practically twins."

The man's face twisted slightly. His lips curled into a faint sneer, and his eyes gazed scornfully at Cemp.

He said in an exact replica of Cemp's baritone voice, "It was my intent that you notice. If you hadn't this first time, then I would have approached you again. My name is U-Brem."

Cemp was silent, startled. He was surprised at the hostility in the stranger's tone and manner. Contempt, he analyzed wonderingly.

Had the man been merely a human being who had somehow recognized a Silkie in human form, Cemp would have considered it one of those occasional incidents. Known Silkies were sometimes sought out by humans and insulted. Usually the human who committed such a foolish act could be evaded or good-naturedly parried or won over. But once in a while a Silkie had to fight. However, the man's resemblance to Cemp indicated that this encounter was different.

As he had these thoughts, the stranger's cynical gray-blue eyes were gazing into Cemp's. The man's lips parted in a derisive smile, showing even white teeth. "At aproximately this moment," he said, "every Silkie in the solar system is receiving a communication from his alter ego."

He paused; again the insolent smile. "I can see that has alerted you, and you're bracing yourself . . ."

It was true. Cemp had abruptly decided that whether the other's statement was true or not, he could not let him get away.

The man continued, ". . . bracing yourself to try to seize me. It can't be done, for I match you in every way."

"You're a Silkie?" Cemp asked.

"I'm a Silkie."

By all the logic of Silkie history, that had to be a false claim. And yet there was the unmistakable, sensational resemblance to himself.

But Cemp did not change his mind. Even if this was a Silkie, Cemp had a superiority over all other Silkies. In his struggle with the Kibmadine the year before, he had learned things about body control that were known to no other Silkie, since it had been decided by the Silkie Authority that he must not communicate to other Silkies the newly gained abilities. And he hadn't.

That extra knowledge would now be to his advantage —if the other was indeed a Silkie.

"Ready for the message?" asked the man insolently.

Cemp, who was ready for the battle of his life, nodded curtly.

"It's an ultimatum."

"I'm waiting," said Cemp.

"You are to cease and desist from your association with human beings. You are commanded to return to the nation of Silkies. You have a week to make up your mind. After that date you will be considered a traitor and will be treated as traitors have always been treated, without mercy."

Since there was no "nation" of Silkies and never had been, Cemp, after considering the unexpected "ultimatum" for a moment, made his attack.

He still didn't quite believe that his "twin" was a Silkie. So he launched a minimum electric charge on one of the magnetic bands that he could use as a human —enough to render unconsciousness but not damage.

To his dismay, a Silkie magnetic screen as powerful as anything he could muster warded off the energy blow. So the man was a Silkie.

The stranger stared at him, teeth showing, eyes glinting with sudden rage. "I'll remember this!" he snarled. "You'd have hurt me if I hadn't had a defense."

Cemp hesitated, questioning his own purpose. It didn't have to be capture. "Look," he urged, "why don't you come with me to the Silkie Authority? If there is a Silkie nation, normal communication is the best way of proving it."

The strange Silkie began to back away. "I've done

my duty," he muttered. "I'm not accustomed to fighting. You tried to kill me."

He seemed to be in a state of shock. His eyes had changed again, and they looked dazed now. All the man's initial cocksureness was gone as he continued backing away.

Cemp followed, uncertain. He was himself a highly trained fighter; it was hard to grasp that here might be a Silkie who was actually not versed in battle.

He soothed, "We don't have to fight. But you can't expect to deliver an ultimatum and then go off into nowhere, as if you've done your part. You say your name is U-Brem. Where do you come from?"

He was aware, as he spoke, that people had stopped in the street and were watching the strange drama of two men, one retreating, the other pursuing, a slow step at a time.

"First, if there's a Silkie nation, where has it—where have you—been hiding all these years?" Cemp persisted.

"Damn you, stop badgering me. You've got your ultimatum. You've got a week to think about it. Now leave me alone!"

The alter ego had clearly not considered what he would do after delivering his message. His unpreparedness made the whole incident even more fantastic. But he was showing anger again, recovering his nerve.

An electric discharge, in the jagged form of lightning, rode a magnetic beam of U-Brem's creation and struck at Cemp, crackling against the magnetic screen he kept ready to be triggered into instant existence.

The lightning bolt bounced away from Cemp, caromed off a building, flashed across the sidewalk past several startled people, and grounded itself on the metal grill of a street drain.

"Two can play that game," said U-Brem in a savage tone.

Cemp made no reply. The other's electric beam had

been maximum for a Silkie in human form—death-level potency. Somewhere nearby, a woman screamed. The street was clearing. People were running away, seeking shelter.

The time had come to end this madness, or someone might be killed. Cemp acted on his evaluation that for some reason that was not clear, this Silkie was not properly trained and was therefore vulnerable to a nonlethal attack by a technique involving a simple version of levels of logic.

He wouldn't even have to use the secret ability he had learned from the Kibmadine the year before.

The moment he made up his mind, he did a subtle energy thing. He modified a specific set of low-energy force lines passing through his brain and going in the direction of U-Brem.

Instantly, there was manifested a strange logic implicit in the very structure and makeup of life. The logic of levels! The science that had been derived by human scientific methods from the great Silkie ability for changing form.

Each life cell had its own rigidity. Each gestalt of cells did a specific action, could do no other. Once stimulated, the "thought" in that particular nerve bundle went through its exact cycle, and if there was an accompanying motion or emotion, that also manifested itself precisely and exactly and without qualification.

Even more meaningful, more important—a number of cell colonies could be joined together to form a new gestalt, and groups of such clusters had *their* special action. One such colony gestalt was the sleep center in human beings.

The method Cemp used wouldn't work on a Silkie in his class-C form. Even a B Silkie could fight off sleep. But this Silkie in human form began to stagger. His eyes were suddenly heavy lidded, and the uncontrolled appearance of his body showed that he was asleep on his feet.

As the man fell, Cemp stepped forward and caught his body, preventing an injurious crash to the concrete sidewalk. Simultaneously, he did a second, subtle thing. On another force line, he put a message that manipulated the unconsciousness gestalt in the other's brain. It was an attempt at complete control. Sleep cut off U-Brem's perception of his environment. Cemp's manipulation of his unconsciousness mechanism eliminated those messages from the brain's stored memory which would normally stimulate to wakefulness someone who was not really sleepy.

Cemp was congratulating himself on his surprisingly easy capture—when the body he held stiffened. Cemp, sensing an outside force, drew back. To his complete astonishment, the unconscious man rose straight up into the sky.

In his human form, Cemp was not able to determine the nature of the energy that could accomplish such an improbable feat. He should, he realized, transform to Silkie. He found himself hesitating. There was a rule against changing in full view of human beings. Abruptly, he recognized that this situation was unique, a never-before-encountered emergency. He transformed to Silkie and cut off gravity.

The ten-foot body, shaped a little like a projectile, rose from the ground at missile speed. Most of his clothes, completely torn away, fell to the ground. A few tattered remnants remained but were swept away by the gale winds created by his passage.

Unfortunately, all of five seconds had gone by while he made the transformation, and since several seconds had already passed before he acted, he found himself pursuing a speck that was continuing to go straight up.

What amazed him anew was that even with his Silkie perception, he could detect no energy from it, below it, or around it. Yet its speed was as great as anything he could manage. Accordingly, after only moments, he realized that his pursuit was not swift enough to overtake the man and that the body of U-Brem would reach an atmosphere height too rarefied for human survival unless he acted promptly. He therefore mercifully removed the pressure from the sleep and unconsciousness center of the other's body.

Moments later, he was disappointed, but not surprised, he sensed from the other a shift to Silkie form; proof that he had awakened and could now be responsible for himself.

U-Brem continued straight up, as a full-grown Silkie now, and it was presently obvious that he intended to risk going through the Van Allen belt. Cemp had no such foolhardy purpose.

As the two of them approached the outer limits of the atmosphere, Cemp put a thought on a beam to a manned Telstar unit in orbit around Earth. The thought contained simply the data about what had happened.

The message sent, he turned back. Greatly disturbed by his experience—and being without clothes for human wear—he flew straight to the Silkie Authority.

# X

CEMP, descending from the sky down to the vast building complex that comprised the central administration for dealing with Silkies, saw that other Silkies were also coming in. He presumed, grimly, that they were there for the same reason as he was.

As the realization came, he scanned the heavens behind him with his Silkie senses and perceived that scores more of black spots were out there, hurtling closer. Divining imminent confusion, he slowed and stopped. Then, from his position in the sky, he telepathed Charley Baxter, proposing a special plan to handle the emergency.

Baxter was in a distracted state, but presently his return thought came. "Nat, yours is just about the best idea we've had. And you're right. This could be dangerous."

There was a pause. Baxter must have got his message through to other of the Special People, for Cemp began to record a general Silkie warning. "To all Silkies: It would be unwise for too many of you to concentrate at one time in one place. So divide into ten groups on the secret-number system, plan G. Group One only, approach and land. All others disperse until called."

In the sky near Cemp, Silkies began to mill around. Cemp, who, by the designated number system, was in group three, veered off, climbed to the upper atmosphere, and darted a thousand miles over, to his home in Florida.

En route, he talked mentally to his wife, Joanne. And so by the time he walked naked into the house, she had clothes laid out for him and knew as much as he about what had happened.

As Cemp dressed, he saw that she was in a womanly state of alarm, more concerned than he. She accepted that there was a Silkie nation and that this meant there would also be Silkie women.

"Admit it!" she said tearfully. "That thought has already crossed your mind, hasn't it?"

"I'm a logical person," Cemp defended. "So I've had fleeting thoughts about all possibilities. But being sensible, I feel that a lot of things have to be explained before I can reject what we know of Silkie history. And so until we have proof of something different, I shall go on believing that Silkies are the result of biological experiments with DNA and DNP and that old Sawyer did it there on Echo Island."

"What's going to become of our marriage?" Joanne said in an anguished voice.

"Nothing will change."

She sobbed. "I'm going to seem to you like a native woman of three hundred years ago who is married to a white man on a South Sea Island—and then white women begin arriving on the island."

The wildness of her fantasying astounded Cemp. "It's not the same," he said. "I promise complete loyalty and devotion for the rest of our lives."

"Nobody can promise anything in personal relations," she said. But his words seemed to reassure her after a moment. She dried her eyes and came over to him and allowed herself to be kissed.

It was an hour before a phone call came from Charley Baxter. The man was apologetic for the delay but explained that it was the result of a conference on Cemp's future actions.

"It was a discussion just about you in all this," Baxter said.

Cemp waited.

The final decision was to continue to not let Cemp

intermingle with other Silkies—"for reasons that you know," Baxter said significantly.

Cemp surmised that the reference was to the secret knowledge he had gained from the Kibmadine Di-isarinn and that this meant they would continue to send him on special missions that kept him away from other Silkies.

Baxter now produced the information that only four hundred Silkies had been approached by alter egos. "The number actually reported in," he said, "is three hundred and ninety-six."

Cemp was vaguely relieved, vaguely contemptuous. U-Brem's claim that all Silkies were targets was now proved to be propaganda. He had already shown himself to be an inept Silkie. The lie added one more degrading touch.

"Some of them were pretty poor duplicates," said Baxter. "Apparently, mimicking another body is not a great skill with them."

However, he admitted, even four hundred was more than enough to establish the existence of a hitherto unknown group of Silkies.

"Even if they are untrained," he said, "we've absolutely got to find out who they are and where they come from."

"Is there no clue?" Cemp asked.

No more than he already knew.

"They all got away?" Cemp said, astounded. "No one did any better than I did?"

"On the average, not as well," said Baxter.

It seemed that most Silkies had made no effort to hold the strange Silkies who confronted them; they had simply reported in and asked for instructions.

"Can't blame them," said Baxter.

He continued, "But I might as well tell you that your fight and your reasons for fighting make you one of the two dozen Silkies we feel we can depend on in this matter. So here are your instructions . . ."

He talked for several minutes and, concluded, "Take Joanne with you, but go at once!"

The sign said, ALL THE MUSIC IN THIS BUILDING IS SILKIE MUSIC.

Cemp, who had never listened for long to any other kind, saw the faint distaste come into his wife's face. She caught his look and evidently his thought, for she said, "All right, so it sounds dead level to me, as if it's all the same note—well, anyway, the same few notes, close together, repeated in various sickening combinations."

She stopped, shook her beautiful blonde head, and said, "I guess I'm tense and afraid and need something wild and clashy."

To Cemp, who could hear harmonies in the music that were beyond the reach of ordinary human ears, her outburst was but a part of the severe emotional reactions to things that Silkies married to human women had to become accustomed to. The wives of Silkies had a hard time making their peace with the realities of the relationship.

As Joanne had put it more than once, "There you are with this physically perfect, beautiful male. But all the time you're thinking, 'This is not really a man. It's a monster that can change in a flash into either a fishlike being or a creature of space.' But of course, I wouldn't part with him for anything."

The music sign was soon behind them, and they walked on into the interior of the museum. Their destination was the original laboratory, in which the first Silkie was supposed to have been produced. The lab occupied the center of the building; it had been moved there from the West Indies a hundred and ten years before, according to a date on a wall plaque at the entrance.

It had seemed to Baxter that a sharper study should

be made of the artifacts of Silkie history. The entire structure of that history was now being questioned for the very first time.

This task, of reevaluating the past data, had been assigned to Cemp and Joanne.

The lab was brightly lighted. It had only one visitor; a rather plain young woman with jet-black hair but no makeup, wearing ill-fitting clothes, was standing at one of the tables beside the far doorway.

As Cemp came in, a thought not his own touched his mind. He started to turn to Joanne, taking it for granted that she had communicated with him on that level. He took it for granted, that is, for several seconds.

Belatedly, realization came that the thought had arrived on a magnetic carrier wave—Silkie level.

Cemp swung around and stared at the black-haired woman. She smiled at him, somewhat tensely, he noted, and then her thought came, unmistakably: "Please don't give me away. I was stationed here to convince any doubting Silkie."

She didn't have to explain what she meant. The thunder of it was pouring through Cemp's mind.

According to his knowledge, there had never been any female Silkies. All Silkies on Earth were males, married to women of the Special People—like Joanne.

But this black-haired, farm-woman type was a female Silkie! That was what she was letting him know by her presence. In effect, by being here, she was saying, "Don't bother to search dusty old files. I'm living proof that Silkies were not produced in somebody's laboratory two hundred and thirty years ago."

Suddenly Cemp was confused. He was aware that Joanne had come up beside him, that she must have caught his thought, that she was herself dismayed. The one glimpse he had of her face showed that she had become very pale.

"Nat!" her voice came sharply. "You've got to capture her!"

Cemp started forward, but it was a half-hearted movement. Yet in spite of the uncertainty in his actions, he was already having logical thoughts.

Since only hours had gone by since the moment he first saw U-Brem, she must have been stationed here in advance. She would therefore have had no contact with the others. And so she wouldn't know that to a trained Silkie like himself, she was as vulnerable as an unarmed civilian opposed by a soldier.

The black-haired woman must have suddenly had some doubt of her own. Abruptly she stepped through the door near which she had been standing and closed it after her.

"Nat!" Joanne's voice, high-pitched, sounded mere inches behind him. "You can't let her get away!"

Cemp, who had emerged from his brief stasis, projected a thought after the female Silkie. "I'm not going to fight you, but I'm going to stay close to you until I have all the information we want."

"Too late!" A magnetic carrier wave, human-Silkie level, brought her thought. "You're already too late."

Cemp didn't think so. He arrived at the door through which she had disappeared, was slightly disconcerted to find that it was locked, smashed it with a single jagged lightning thrust of electrical force, stepped through its smoking remains—and saw the woman in the act of entering a gap in the wall made by a sliding door.

She was not more than three dozen feet away, and she had half-turned to look back in his direction. What she saw was evidently a surprise, for a startled look came into her face.

Hastily, her hand came up to something inside the aperture, and the door slid shut. As it closed, Cemp, who was running toward it, had a glimpse of a gleaming corridor beyond. The existence of such a secret passageway had too many implications for Cemp to consider immediately.

He was at the wall, fumbling for the hidden door. When he could not find it after several long moments, he stepped back and burned it down with the two energy flows from his brain, which, when they came together outside his body, created an intense electrical arc. It was the only energy weapon available to him as a human being, but it was enough.

A minute later, he stepped through the smoking opening into a narrow corridor.

## XI

THE CORRIDOR in which Cemp found himself was made of concrete and slanted gently downward. It was dimly lighted and straight, and he could see the young woman in the near distance ahead—about two hundred feet away.

She was running, but as a woman wearing a dress runs—not very fast. Cemp broke into his own high-speed lope and in a minute had cut the distance between them in half. Abruptly, the concrete ended. Ahead was a dirt cave, still lighted, but the lights were set farther apart.

As she reached this point, the young woman sent him a message on a magnetic force line. "If you don't stop chasing me, I'll have to use the [something not clear to Cemp] power."

Cemp remembered the energy that had lifted U-Brem into the sky. He took the threat seriously and instantly modified a magnetic wave to render her unconscious.

It was not so cruel an act as it would have been earlier. Now she fell like a stone—which was the unfortunate characteristic of the unconsciousness gestalt—but she fell on dirt and not on cement. The motion of her body was such that she pitched forward on her knees, then slid down on her right shoulder. It didn't look too severe for her—so it seemed to Cemp as he came closer to where she was lying.

He had slowed to a walk. Now, still wary, he approached the prostrate body, determined not to let any special "power" remove her from him. He felt only slightly guilty at the violent method he had used. His reasoning had permitted no less control over her. The "sleep" shut-off on U-Brem had not prevented that individual from turning on the force field—so Cemp considered it to be—that had saved him. Quite simply, he couldn't let her get away.

Because it was an untried situation, he acted at once. At this moment, he had her; there were too many unknowns for him to risk any delay. He knelt beside her. Since she was unconscious and not asleep, her sensory system was open to exterior stimulation. But for her to answer, she would have to be switched to sleep, so that the shut-off interior perception could flow.

So he sat there, alternately manipulating her unconsciousness center, when he wanted to ask a question, and her sleep center, for her reply. It was like ancient ham radio with each party saying "over" when his message was completed.

And of course, in addition, he had to make sure that she did reply to his queries. So he asked one question after another, and with each question he modified a magnetic wave with a message to the brain-cell gestalt that responded to hypnotic drugs. The result was a steady mental conversation.

"What is your name?"

"B-Roth."

"Where do you come from?"

"From home."

"Where is home?"

"In the sky." A mental image came of a small stone body in space; Cemp's impression was of a meteorite less than twenty miles in diameter. "About to go around the sun, inside the first planet's orbit."

So she *had* come to Earth in advance. So they *were* all far from "home" and had apparently had no preliminary knowledge that they were outskilled by Earth Silkies. As a result, he was now obtaining this decisive information.

"What is its orbit?" Cemp asked.

"It goes as far out as the eighth planet."

Neptune! What a tremendous distance—nearly thirty astronomical units.

Cemp asked quickly, "What is its mean speed?"

Her answer was in terms of Mercury's year. Converted to Earth time, it came to a hundred and ten years per orbit.

Cemp whistled softly. An immediate association had leaped into his mind. The first Silkie baby had been born to Marie Ederle slightly more than two hundred and twenty years before, according to the official history. The time involved was approximately twice as long as the orbital period of the little Silkie planetoid.

Cemp ended that train of speculation abruptly and demanded from B-Roth exactly how she would again find the planetoid, which surely must be one of thousands of similar bodies.

The answer was one that only a Silkie could operate from. She had in her brain a set of relationships and signal-recognition images that identified for her the location of the Silkie home.

Cemp made an exact mental copy of these images. He was about to begin questioning her for details on other matters—when an inertia phenomenon effected his body.

He was flung backward. . . . It was as if he were in a vehicle, his back to the forward motion, and the vehicle stopped suddenly, but he went on.

Because he always had protection against sudden falls, he had been moved less than eight feet before he triggered his magnetic field, his only screening mechanism as a human.

The field he set up could not stop the pull of gravity directly, but it derived from the Earth's magnetic force and gained its power from the force lines that passed through this exact space.

As Cemp modulated the lines now, they attached

themselves to flexible metal bands that were woven into his clothes, and they held him. He hung there a few feet above the floor. From this vantage point he was able to examine his situation.

At once, the phenomenon was shown as completely fantastic. He detected in the heart of the gravity field a tiny molecule complex. What was fantastic about it was this: Gravity was an invariable, solely dependent on mass and square of distance. Cemp had already calculated the gravity pull on him to be the equivalent of three times that of Earth at sea level. And so, by all the laws of physics, that incredibly small particle must have an equivalent mass to three Earths!

Impossible, of course.

It was by no means a complex of one of the large molecules, as far as Cemp could determine, and it was not radioactive.

He was about to abandon his study of it and to turn his attention to his own situation, when he noticed that the gravity field had an even more improbable quality. Its pull was limited to organic matter. It had no effect on the surrounding dirt walls, and in fact—his mind poised in a final amazement—the woman's body was not influenced by it.

The gravity was limited to one particular organic configuration—himself! One body, one human being only—Nat Cemp—was the sole object toward which it was oriented.

He found himself remembering how he had been untouched by the field that had lifted U-Brem. He had sensed the presence of a field but only by the way the magnetic lines that passed through his head were affected by it. Even in his Silkie form, as he pursued the hurtling body of his alter ego, that, and merely that, had been true.

This was for him a personal gravitational field, a small group of molecules that "knew" him.

As these flashing awarenesses came to him, Cemp turned his head and gazed back at the young woman. He was not surprised at what he saw. His attention had been forcibly removed from her, so the pressure on the unconsciousness valve in her brain was released. She was stirring, coming to.

She sat up, looked around, and saw him.

She came to her feet quickly, with an athletic ease. She evidently did not remember what had happened while she was unconscious, did not realize how completely she had given away basic secrets, for her face broke into a smile.

"You see?" she said. "I told you what would happen. Well, goodbye."

Her spirits visibly high, she turned, walked off into the cave, and presently disappeared as it gradually curved off to the left.

After she was gone, Cemp turned his attention back to the gravity field. He assumed that it would eventually be withdrawn or fade out, and he would be free. He had the distinct conviction that he might have only minutes in which to examine it and discover its nature.

He thought unhappily, *If I could change into my Silkie form, I could really examine it.*

But he dared not, could not. At least, he couldn't do it and simultaneously maintain his safe position.

Silkies had one weakness, if it could be called that. They were vulnerable when they changed from one form to another. Considering this, Cemp now conducted his first mental conversation with Joanne. He explained his predicament, described what he had learned, and ended, "I think I can stay here all day and see what comes of this, but I should probably have another Silkie stand by for emergencies."

Her anxious reply was, "I'll have Charley Baxter contact you."

# XII

SHE PHONED Baxter and passed the conversation on to Cemp in thought form.

Baxter was enormously excited by the information that Cemp had obtained about the alien Silkies. He regarded the gravity field as a new energy application, but he was reluctant to send in another Silkie.

"Let's face it, Joanne," he said. "Your husband learned something last year which, if other Silkies understood it, might wreck the delicate balance by which we are maintaining our present Silkie-human civilization. Nat understands our concern about that. So tell him I'll send a machine in there to act as a barrier for him while he makes his changeover into Silkie.

It occurred to Cemp that the appearance of new, hitherto unknown Silkies would alter the Silkie-human relationship even more. But he did not permit that thought to go out to Joanne.

Baxter's conversation concluded with the statement that it would probably take a while before the machine could be got to him. "So tell him to hold on."

After Baxter had hung up, Joanne thought at Cemp, "I should tell you that I am relieved about one thing."

"What's that?"

"If the Silkie women are all as plain in human form as B-Roth, then I'm not going to worry."

An hour went by. Two . . . ten.

In the world outside, the skies would be dark, the sun long gone, the stars signaling in their tiny brilliant fashion.

Charley Baxter's machine had come and gone, and Cemp, safe in the Silkie form, remained close to the

73

most remarkable energy field that had ever been seen in the solar system. What was astounding was that it showed no diminution of its colossal gravity effect. His hope had been that with his supersensitive Silkie perception he would be able to perceive any feeder lines that might be flowing power to it from an outside source. But there was nothing like that; nothing to trace. The power came from the single small group of molecules. It had no other origin.

The minutes and the hours lengthened. The watch became long, and he had time to feel the emotional impact of the problem that now confronted every Silkie on Earth—the need to make a decision about the Space Silkies.

Morning.

Shortly after the sun came up outside, the field manifested an independent quality. It began to move along the corridor, heading deeper into the cave. Cemp floated along after it, letting a portion of its gravitational pull draw him. He was wary but curious, hopeful that now he would find out more.

The cave ended abruptly in a deep sewer, which had the look of long abandonment. The concrete was cracked, and there were innumerable deep fissures in the walls. But to the group of molecules and their field, it seemed to be a familiar area, for they went forward more rapidly. Suddenly, there was water below them. It was not stagnant, but rippled and swirled. A tidal pool, Cemp analyzed.

The water grew deeper, and presently they were in it, traveling at undiminished speed. Ahead, the murky depths grew less murky. They emerged into sunlit waters in a canyon about a hundred feet below the surface of the ocean.

As they broke surface a moment later, the strange energy complex accelerated. Cemp, suspecting that it would now try to get away from him, made a final effort to perceive its characteristics.

But nothing came back to him. No message, no sign of energy flow. For a split second, he did have the impression that the atoms making up the molecule group were somehow . . . not right. But when he switched his attention to the band involved, either the molecules became aware of his momentary awareness and closed themselves off or he imagined it.

Even as he made the analysis, his feeling that he was about to be discarded was borne out. The particle's speed increased rapidly. In seconds, its velocity approached the limits of what he could permit himself to endure inside an atmosphere. The outer chitin of his Silkie body grew hot, then hotter.

Reluctantly, Cemp adjusted his own atomic structure, so that the gravity of the alien field no longer affected him. As he fell away, it continued to pursue a course that took an easterly direction, where the sun was now about an hour above the horizon. Within mere seconds of his separation from it, it left the atmosphere and, traveling at many miles a second, headed seemingly straight for the sun.

Cemp came to the atmosphere's edge. "Gazing" by means of his Silkie perceptors out upon the vast, dark ocean of space beyond, he contacted the nearest Telstar unit. To the scientists aboard, he gave a fix on the speeding molecule group. Then he waited hopefully while they tried to put a tracer on it.

But the word finally came, "Sorry, we get no reaction."

Baffled, Cemp let himself be drawn by Earth's gravity. Then, by a series of controlled adjustments to the magnetic and gravity fields of the planet, he guided himself to the Silkie Authority.

# XIII

THREE HOURS of talk . . .

Cemp, who, as the only Silkie present, occupied a seat near the foot of the long table, found the discussion boring.

It had early seemed to him that he or some other Silkie ought to be sent to the Silkie planetoid to learn the facts, handle the matter in a strictly logical but humanitarian fashion, and report back to the Authority.

If, for some reason, the so-called Silkie nation proved unamenable to reason, then a further discussion would be in order.

As he waited for the three dozen human conferees to reach the same decision, he couldn't help but notice the order of importance at the table.

The Special People, including Charley Baxter, were at the head of the long table. Next, ranging down on either side, were the ordinary human beings. Then, on one side, himself, and below him, three minor aides and the official secretary of the three-man Silkie Authority.

It was not a new observation for him. He had discussed it with other Silkies, and it had been pointed out to him that here was a reversal of the power role that was new in history. The strongest individuals in the solar system—the Silkies—were still relegated to secondary status.

He emerged from his reverie to realize that silence had fallen. Charley Baxter, slim, gray-eyed, intense, was coming around the long table. He stopped across from Cemp.

"Well, Nat," said Baxter, "there's the picture as we see it." He seemed embarrassed.

76

Cemp did a lightning mental backtrack on the discussion and realized that they had indeed arrived at the inevitable conclusion. But he noted also that they considered it a weighty decision. It was a lot to ask of any person, that was the attitude. The result could be personal disaster. They wouldn't be critical if he refused.

"I feel ashamed to ask it," said Baxter, "but this is almost a war situation."

Cemp could see that they were not sure of themselves. There had been no war on Earth for a hundred and fifty years. No one was an expert in it any more.

He climbed to his feet as these awarenesses touched him. Now he looked around at the faces turned to him and said, "Calm yourselves, gentlemen. Naturally I'll do it."

They all looked relieved. The discussion turned quickly to details—the difficulty of locating a single meteorite in space, particularly one that had such a long sidereal period.

It was well-known that there were about fifteen hundred large meteorites and planetoids and tens of thousands of smaller objects orbiting the sun. All these had orbits or motions that, though subject to the laws of celestial mechanics, were often very eccentric. A few of them, like comets, periodically came in close to the sun, then shot off into space again, returning for another hectic go-round fifty to a hundred years later. There were so many of these intermediate-sized rocks that they were identified and their courses plotted only for special reasons. There had simply never been any point in tracking them all.

Cemp had matched course with and landed on scores of lone meteorites. His recollections of those experiences were among the bleaker memories of his numerous space flights—the darkness, the sense of utterly barren rock, the profound lack of sensory stimulation. Oddly, the larger they were, the worse the feeling was.

He had discovered that he could have a kind of intellectual affinity with a rock less than a thousand feet in diameter. This was particularly true when he encountered an inarticulate mass that had finally been precipitated into a hyperbolic orbit. When he computed that it was thus destined to leave the solar system forever, he would find himself imaging how long it had been in space, how far it had gone, and how it would now hurtle away from the solar system and spend eons between the stars, he could not help feeling a sense of loss.

A government representative—a human being named John Mathews—interrupted his thought. "Mr. Cemp, I'd like to ask you a very personal question."

Cemp looked at him and nodded.

The man went on, "According to reports, several hundred Earth Silkies have already defected to these native Silkies. Evidently, you don't feel as they do, that the Silkie planetoid is home. Why not?"

Cemp smiled. "Well, first of all," he said, "I would never buy a pig in a poke the way they have done."

He hesitated. Then, in a serious tone, he continued, "Entirely apart from my feelings of loyalty to Earth, I do not believe the future of life forms will be helped or advanced by any rigid adherence to the idea that I am a lion, or I am a bear. Intelligent life is, or should be, moving toward a common civilization. Maybe I'm like the farm boy who went to the city—Earth. Now my folks want me to come back to the farm. They'll never understand why I can't, so I don't even try to explain it to them."

"Maybe," said Mathews, "the planetoid is actually the big city and Earth the farm. What then?"

Cemp smiled politely but merely shook his head.

Mathews persisted, "One more question. How should Silkies be treated?"

Cemp spread his hands. "I can't think of a single change that would be of value."

He meant it. He had never been able to get excited about the pecking order. Yet he had known for a long time that some Silkies felt strongly about their inferior —as it seemed to them—role. Others, like himself, did their duty, were faithful to their human wives, and tried to enjoy the somewhat limited possibilities of human civilization—limited for Silkies, who had so many additional senses for which there was no real creative stimulation.

Presumably, things could be better. But meanwhile, they were what they were. Cemp recognized that any attempt to alter them would cause fear and disturbance among human beings. And why do that merely to satisfy the egos of somewhat fewer than two thousand Silkies?

At least, that had been the problem until now. The coming of the space Silkies would add an indefinite number of new egos to the scene, yet, Cemp reasoned, not enough to change the statistics meaningfully.

Aloud, he said, "As far as I can see, under all conceivable circumstances, there is no better solution to the Silkie problem than that which exists right now."

Charley Baxter chose that moment to end the discussion, saying, "Nat, you have our best, our very best, wishes. And our complete confidence. A spaceship will rush you to Mercury's orbit and give you a head start. Good luck."

# XIV

THE SCENE ahead was absolutely fantastic.

The Silkie planetoid would make its circuit of the sun far inside Mercury's eccentric orbit, and the appearance was that it might brush the edges of the great clouds of hot gas that seemed to poke out like streamers or shapeless arms from the sun's hot surface.

Cemp doubted if such a calamity would actually occur, but as he periodically subjected his steel-hard chitinous Silkie body to the sun's gravity, he sensed the enormous pull of it at this near distance. The circle of white fire filled almost the entire sky ahead. The light was so intense and came in on him on so many bands that it overwhelmed his receptor system whenever he let it in. And he had to open up at intervals in order to make readjustments in his course.

The two hurtling bodies—his own and that of the planetoid—were presently on a collision course. The actual moment of "collision" was still hours away. So Cemp shut off his entire perception system. Thus, instantly, he sank into the deep sleep that Silkies so rarely allowed themselves.

He awoke in stages and saw that his timing had been exact. The planetoid was now "visible" on one of the tiny neural screens inside the forward part of his body. It showed as a radar-type image, and at the beginning it was the size of a pea.

In less than thirty minutes it grew to an apparent size of five miles, which was half its diameter, he estimated.

At this point, Cemp performed his only dangerous maneuver. He allowed the sun's gravity to draw him between the sun and the planetoid. Then he cut off the sun's gravity and, using a few bursts of energy manufactured at the edge of a field behind his body, darted toward the planetoid's surface.

What was dangerous about this action was that it brought him in on the dayside. With the superbrilliant sunlight behind him, he was clearly visible to anyone in or on or around the planetoid. But his theory was that no Silkie would normally be exposing himself to the sun, that in fact, every sensible Silkie would be inside the big stone ball or on its night side.

At close range in that ultrabright light, the planetoid looked like the wrinkled head and face of a bald old Amerind. It was reddish-gray and pock marked and lined and not quite round. The pock marks turned out to be actual caves. Into one of these, Cemp floated. He went down into what to human eyes would have been pitch darkness, but the interior was visible to him as a Silkie on many bands.

He found himself in a corridor with smooth granite walls that led slantingly downward. After about twenty minutes he came to a turn in the passageway. As he rounded it, he saw a shimmering, almost opaque energy screen in front of him.

Cemp decided at once not to regard it as a problem. He doubted if it had been put up to catch anyone. In fact, his lightning analysis of it indicated that it was a wall, with the equivalent solidity of a large spaceship's outer skin.

As a screen it was strong enough to keep out the most massive armor-piercing shells. Going through such a screen was an exercise in Silkie energy control. First, he put up a matching field and started it oscillating. The oscillation unstabilized the opposing screen and started it in a sympathetic vibration. As the process continued, the screen and the field began to merge. But it was the screen that became part of Cemp's field, not the reverse.

Thus, his field was within minutes a part of the barrier. Safely inside his field, he crossed the barrier space. Once past it, disengagement was a matter of slowing down the oscillation until the field and the screen abruptly became separate entities.

The sound of the separation was like the crack of a whip, and the presence of sound indicated he had come into air space. Quickly, he discovered that it was air of an unearthly mixture—thirty percent oxygen, twenty percent helium, and most of the rest gaseous sulphur compounds.

The pressure was about twice that of sea level on Earth, but it was air, and it undoubtedly had a purpose.

From where he had floated through the energy barrier, he saw a large chamber the floor of which was about a hundred feet below him.

Soft lights shone down. Seen in their light, the room was a jewel. The walls were inlaid with precious stones, fine metals, and vari-colored rock cunningly cut into a design. The design was a continuing story picture of a race of four-legged centaur-type beings with a proud bearing and—wherever there were close-ups—sensitive though nonhuman faces.

On the floor was a picture of a planet inset in some kind of glowing substance that showed the curving, mountainous surface, with sparkling lines where rivers flowed, likenesses of forests and other growth, glinting oceans and lakes, and thousands of bright spots marking cities and towns.

The sides of the planet curved away in proper proportion, and Cemp had the feeling that the globe continued on down and that the bottom was probably visible in some lower room.

The overall effect was completely and totally *beautiful*.

Cemp surmised that the life scenes and the planet picture were an accurate eidolon of a race and a place with which the Silkies had at some time in their past been associated.

He was mentally staggered by the artistic perfection of the room.

He had already, as he floated down, noticed that there were large archways leading to adjoining chambers. He had glimpses of furniture, machines, objects, shining bright and new. He surmised they were artifacts of either the centaur or other civilizations. But he could not take time to explore. His attention fastened on a stairway that led down to the next level.

He went down it and presently found himself facing another energy barrier. Penetrating it exactly as he had the other, he moved on and into a chamber filled with sea water. Inset in the floor of that huge room was a planet that glimmered with the green-blue of an undersea civilization.

And that was only the beginning. Cemp went down from one level to another, each time through an energy screen and through a similarly decorated chamber. Each was inlaid in the same way with precious stones and glinting metals. Each had breathtaking scenes from what he presumed were habitable planets of far stars, and each had a different atmosphere.

After a dozen such chambers, Cemp found that the impact was cumulative. Realization came to him that here, inside this planetoid, had been gathered such treasure as probably did not exist anywhere else. Cemp visualized the seven hundred-odd cubic miles that comprised the interior of the most fantastic asteroid in the galaxy, and he remembered what Mathews had said—that perhaps the planetoid was the "city" and Earth was the "farm."

It began to seem that the man's speculation might be truth.

He had been expecting to collide momentarily with an inhabitant of the planetoid. After passing three more chambers, each with its glowing duplicate in miniature of a planet of long ago and far away, Cemp paused and reconsidered.

He had a strong feeling that in learning of these treasures, he had gained an advantage—which he must not lose—and that the Silkies did indeed have their living quarters on the side away from the sun and that they did not expect anyone to arrive in this surprise fashion.

The idea continued to seem correct, and so he turned back and was presently dropping directly toward the dark side. Again the cave openings and, a few score feet inside, the energy barrier. Beyond that were air and gravitation exactly like those at sea level on Earth.

Cemp floated down into a smoothly polished granite chamber. It was furnished with settees, chairs, and tables, and there was a long, low-built bookcase at one end. But the arrangement was like that in an anteroom —formal and unlived in. It gave him an eerie feeling.

Still in his Silkie form, he went down a staircase and into another chamber. It had soil in it, and there was vegetation, which consisted of temperate-zone Earth shrubs and flowers. Once more, the arrangement was formal.

On the third level down were Earthlike offices, with information computers. Cemp, who understood such matters, recorded what they were. He observed also that no one was using this particular source of data.

He was about to go down to the next level, when an energy beam of enormous power triggered the superfast defense screen he had learned from the Kibmadine.

The coruscation as the beam interacted, in an ever-vaster intensity, with Cemp's barrier screen lit the chamber as if sunlight had suddenly been let in. It stayed lit as whoever was directing the beam tested the screen's durability in a sustained power thrust.

For Cemp, it was a fight that moved at lightning

speed down the entire line of his defenses and came finally up against the hard core of the second method the Kibmadine had taught him.

There, and only there, he held his own.

# XV

A MINUTE went by before the attacker finally seemed to accept that Cemp simply used the beam itself to maintain the barrier. Hence, it took nothing out of him, and the barrier would last as long as the beam did, re-forming as often as necessary.

As suddenly as it had begun, the attacking energy ceased.

Cemp stared around him, dismayed. The entire chamber was a shambles of twisted, white-hot machinery and debris. The granite walls had crumbled, exposing raw meteorite rock. Molten rock dripped in a score of flowing rivers from the shattered ceiling and walls. Great sections were still tumbling and sliding.

What had been a modern office had become in a matter of minutes a gutted desolation of blackened metal and rock.

For Cemp, the initial staggering reality was that only the high-speed Kibmadine screen had saved him. The assault had been gauged to overwhelm and overspeed the entire Silkie defense and attack system.

The intent had been death. No bargaining, no discussion, no questions.

The hard fight had driven him down to a special logic of levels. He felt an automatic outflow of hatred.

Yet after a little, another realization penetrated. *I won!* he thought.

Calm again but savage, he went down five more levels and emerged abruptly at the upper level of a great vista, a huge open space. The city of the space Silkies spread below him.

It was precisely and exactly a small Earth city—apartment buildings, private residences, tree-lined streets. Cemp was bemused, for here, too, the native Silkies had clearly attempted to create a human atmosphere.

He could make out figures on a sidewalk far below. He started down. When he was a hundred feet above them, the people stopped and looked up at him. One— a woman—directed a startled thought at him. "Who are you?"

Cemp told her.

The reaction of the four nearest people was astonishment. But they were not afraid or hostile.

The little group, three women and one man, waited for him. As Cemp came down, he was aware that they were signaling to others. Soon a crowd had gathered, mostly in human bodies, mostly women, but an even dozen arrived in Silkie form.

Guards? he wondered. But they were not antagonistic either. Everybody was mentally open, and what was disconcerting about that was, no one showed any awareness of the attack that had been made on him in the office section near the surface.

Instantly, he saw their unawareness as an opportunity. By keeping silent and alert, he would be able to spot his vicious assailant. He presumed that the violence had been planned and carried out at the administrative level.

*I'll find those so and sos!* he thought grimly.

To his audience of innocent citizens, he said, "I'm acting as an emissary of the Earth Government. My purpose here is to discover what binding agreements are possible."

A woman called up to him, "We can't seem to change into attractive females, Earth-style. What do you suggest?"

A gale of laughter greeted her remark. Cemp was taken aback. He hadn't expected such easy friendliness from the crowd. But his determination did not waver.

"I presume we can discuss that at government level," he said, "but it won't be first on the agenda."

Some remnants of his hate flow must have gone out to them with this thought, for a man said sharply, "He doesn't sound very friendly."

A woman added quickly, "Come now, Mr. Cemp. This is your real home."

Cemp had recovered. He replied in a steady, level thought, "You'll get what you give. Right now, you're giving good. But the agents your government sent to Earth made bloodthirsty threats."

His thought paused there, puzzled. For these people as they were right now did not seem to have any of that threat in them. It struck him that that should be very significant.

After a moment's hesitation, he finished, "I'm here to discover what it's all about, so why not direct me to someone in authority?"

"We don't have authorities." That was a woman.

A man said, "Mr. Cemp, we live a completely free existence here, and you and other Earth Silkies are invited to join us."

Cemp persisted, "Who decided to send those four hundred messengers to Earth?"

"We always do that, when the time comes," another woman replied.

"Complete with threats?" asked Cemp. "Threats of death?"

The woman seemed suddenly uncertain. She turned to one of the men. "You were down there," she said. "Did you threaten violence?"

The man hesitated. "It's a little vague," he said, "but I guess so." He added quickly, "It's always been this way when E-Lerd conditions us in connection with the Power. Memory tends to fade very quickly. In fact, I hadn't recalled that threat aspect until now." He seemed astonished. "I'll be damned. I think we'd better speak to E-Lerd and find the reason for it."

Cemp telepathed directly to the man, "What was your afterfeeling about what you had done?"

"Just that I communicated that we space Silkies were here and that it was time for the Earth Silkies to become aware of their true origin."

He turned to the others. "This is incredible," he said. "I'm astounded. We need to look into E-Lerd's administration of the Power. I uttered murderous words when I was on Earth! That's not like me at all."

His complete amazement was more convincing than anything else could possibly have been.

Cemp said firmly, "I gather, then, that contrary to your earlier statements, you do have a leader and his name is E-Lerd."

One of the Silkies answered that. "No, he's not a leader, but I can see how that might be understood. We're free. No one tells us what to do. But we do delegate responsibilities. For example, E-Lerd is in charge of the Power, and we get its use through him. Would you like to talk to him, Mr. Cemp?"

"Indeed I would," said Cemp with intense satisfaction.

He was thinking, *The Power! Of course. Who else? The person who has control of the Power is the only one who could have attacked me!*

"My name is O-Vedd," said the space Silkie. "Come with me."

His long, bulletlike body detached itself from the group of similar bodies and darted off over the heads of the crowd. Cemp followed. They came down to a small entrance and into a narrow, smooth-walled granite corridor. After a hundred feet this opened out to another huge space. Here was a second city.

At least, for a moment that was what it looked like.

Then Cemp saw that the buildings were of a different character—not dwellings at all. For him, who was familiar with most of the paraphernalia of manufactured energy, there was no question. Some of the massive structures below were the kind that housed atomic power. Others were distributing plants for electricity. Still others had the unmistakable shape of the Ylem transformation systems.

None of these, of course, was *the* Power, but here indeed was power in abundance.

Cemp followed O-Vedd down to the courtyard of a building complex that, despite all its shields, he had no difficulty in identifying as a source of magnetic beams.

The space Silkie landed and transformed to human form, then stood and waited for Cemp to do likewise.

"Nothing doing!" said Cemp curtly. "Ask him to come out here."

O-Vedd shrugged. As a human he was short and dark. He walked off and vanished into a doorway.

Cemp waited amid a silence that was broken only by the faint hum of power from the buildings. A breeze touched the supersensitive spy-ray extensions that he maintained in operation under all circumstances. The little wind registered through the spy mechanism but did not trigger the defense screens behind it.

It was only a breeze, after all, and he had never programmed himself to respond to such minor signals. He was about to dismiss it from his mind, about to contemplate his reaction to the space Silkies—he liked the crowd he had seen—when he thought sharply, A *breeze* here!

Up went his screen. Out projected his perceptors. He had time to notice, then, that it was indeed a breeze but that it was being stirred by a blankness in the surrounding space. Around Cemp, the courtyard grew hazy; then it faded.

There was no planetoid.

Cemp increased all signal sensitivity to maximum. He continued to float in the vacuum of space, and off to one side was the colossal white circle that was the sun. Suddenly, he felt energy drain from his body. The sensation was of his Silkie screens going up, of his system resisting outside energy at many levels.

He thought in tense dismay, *I'm in a fight. It's another attempt to kill me.*

Whatever it was, it was automatic. His own perception remained cut off, and he was impelled to experience what the attacker wanted him to.

Cemp felt like a man suddenly set upon in pitch darkness. But what was appalling about it was that his senses were being held by other forces, preventing awareness of the nature of the attack. What he saw was—

Distance disappeared!

There, spread over many miles of space, was a group of Silkies. Cemp saw them clearly, counted in his lightning fashion two hundred and eighty-eight, caught their thoughts, and recognized that these were the renegade Silkies from Earth.

Suddenly, he understood that they had been told where the Silkie planetoid was and were on their way "home."

Time was telescoped.

The entire group of Silkies was transported in what seemed an instant to within a short distance of the planetoid. Cemp could see the planetoid in the near distance—only a few miles away, twenty at the maximum.

But to him the baffling, deadly, fantastic thing was that as these marvelous events ran their course at one level of his perception, at another level the feeling remained that a determined attempt was being made to kill him.

He could see, feel, be aware of almost nothing. But throughout, the shadowy sensations continued. His energy fields were going through defensive motions. But it was all far away from his awareness, like a human dream.

Being a fully trained Silkie, Cemp watched the internal as well as the external developments with keen observation, strove instant by instant to grasp the reality, monitored incoming signals by the thousands.

He began to sense meaning and to formulate initial speculations about the nature of the physical-world phenomenon involved. And he had the feeling of being on the verge of his first computation, when, as suddenly as it had begun, it ended.

The space scene began to fade. Abruptly, it winked out.

He was back in the courtyard of the buildings that housed the magnetic-power complex. Coming toward him from the open doorway of the main building was O-Vedd. He was accompanied by a man who was of Cemp's general human build—over six feet and strongly muscled. His face was heavier than Cemp's, and his eyes were brown instead of gray.

As he came near, he said, "I am E-Lerd. Let's talk."

# XVI

"To BEGIN with, I want to tell you the history of the Silkies," E-Lerd said.

Cemp was electrified by the statement. He had been braced for a bitter quarrel, and he could feel in himself a multitude of readjusting energy flows . . . proof of the severity of the second all-out fight he had been in. And he absolutely required a complete explanation for the attacks on him.

At that moment, caught up as he was in a steely rage, nothing else could have diverted his attention. But . . . the history of the Silkies! To Cemp, it was instantly the most important subject in the universe.

The Silkie planetoid, E-Lerd began, had entered the solar system from outer space nearly three hundred years before. It had, in due course, been drawn into a Sol-Neptunian orbit. On its first encirclement of the Sun, Silkies visited the inner planets and found that Earth alone was inhabited.

Since they could change form, they studied the biological structure necessary to function in the two atmospheres of Earth—air and water—and set up an internal programming for that purpose.

Unfortunately, a small percentage of the human population, it was soon discovered, could tune in on the thoughts of Silkies. All those who did so in this first visit were quickly hunted down and their memories of the experience blotted out.

But because of these sensitive humans, it became necessary for Silkies to seem to be the product of human biological experiments. An interrelationship with human females was accordingly programmed into Silkies, so that the human female ovum and the male Silkie sperm would produce a Silkie who knew nothing of Silkie history.

In order to maintain this process on an automatic level, the Special People—those persons who could read Silkie minds—were maneuvered into being in charge of it.

Thereupon, all but one of the adult Silkies returned to their planetoid, which now went to the remote end of its orbit. When it came again into the vicinity of Earth, more than a hundred years later, cautious visits were made.

It became apparent that several unplanned things had happened. Human biologists had experimented with the process. As a result, in the early stages, variants had been born. These had propagated their twisted traits and were continuing to do so, growing ever more numerous.

The actual consequences were: a number of true Silkies, capable of making the three-fold transformation at will; class-B Silkies, who could transform from human to fish state, but could not become space people and a stable form: Variants!

The last two groups had largely taken to the oceans. Accordingly it was decided to leave the class-B Silkies alone but to make an effort to inveigle Variants into gigantic spaceships filled with water where they would be isolated and prevented from interbreeding.

This plan was already underway by the time the Silkie planetoid made its round of the sun and again headed out toward far Neptune.

Now they were back, and they had found an unfortunate situation. Somehow, Earth science, virtually ignored by the early visitors, had achieved a method for training the Silkie perception system.

The Earth Silkies had become a loyal-to-Earth, tight-knit, masterful group of beings, lacking only the Power.

Cemp "read" all this in E-Lerd's thought, and then, because he was amazed, he questioned him about what seemed a major omission in his story. Where had the Silkie planetoid come from?

E-Lerd showed his first impatience. "These journeys are too far," he telepathed. "They take too long. Nobody remembers origins. Some other star system, obviously."

"Are you serious?" Cemp was astounded. "You don't know?"

But that was the story. Pry at it as he might, it did not change. Although E-Lerd's mind remained closed except for his telepathed thoughts, O-Vedd's mind was open. In it Cemp saw the same beliefs and the same lack of information.

But why the tampering with human biology and the intermixing of the two breeds?

"We always do that. That's how we live—in a relationship with the inhabitants of a system."

"How do you know you always do that? You just told me you can't remember where you came from this time or where you were before that."

"Well . . . it's obvious from the artifacts we brought along."

E-Lerd's attitude dismissed the questions as being irrelevant. Cemp detected a mind phenomenon in the other that explained the attitude. To space Silkies, the past was unimportant. Silkies *always* did certain things, because that was the way they were mentally, emotionally, and physically constructed.

A Silkie didn't have to know from past experience. He simply had to *be* what was innate in Silkies.

It was, Cemp realized, a basic explanation for much that he had observed. This was why these Silkies had never been trained scientifically. Training was an alien concept in the cosmos of the space Silkies.

"You mean," he protested, incredulous, "you have no

idea why you left the last system where you had this interrelationship with the race there? Why not stay forever in some system where you have located yourself?"

"Probably," said E-Lerd, "somebody got too close to the secret of the Power. That could not be permitted."

That was the reason, he continued, why Cemp and other Silkies had to come back into the fold. As Silkies, they might learn about the Power.

The discussion had naturally come around to *that* urgent subject.

"What," said Cemp, "is the Power?"

E-Lerd stated formally that that was a forbidden subject.

"Then I shall have to force the secret from you," said Cemp. "There can be no agreement without it."

E-Lerd replied stiffly that any attempt at force would require him to use the Power as a defense.

Cemp lost patience. "After your two attempts to kill me," he telepathed in a steely rage, "I'll give you thirty seconds—"

"What attempts to kill you?" said E-Lerd, surprised.

At that precise moment, as Cemp was bracing himself to use logic of levels, there was an interruption.

An "impulse" band—a very low, slow vibration—touched one of the receptors in the forward part of his brain. It operated at mere multiples of the audible sound range directly on his sound-receiving system.

What was new was that the sound acted as a carrier for the accompanying thought. The result was as if a voice spoke clearly and loudly into his ears.

"You win," said the voice. "You have forced me. I shall talk to you myself—bypassing my unknowing servants."

# XVII

CEMP IDENTIFIED the incoming thought formation as a direct contact. Accordingly, his brain, which was programmed to respond instantaneously to a multitude of signals, was triggered into an instant effort to suction more impulses from the sending brain . . . and he got a picture. A momentary glimpse, so brief that even after a few seconds it was hard to be sure that it was real and not a figment of fantasy.

Something huge lay in the darkness deep inside the planetoid. It lay there and gave forth with an impression of vast power. It had been withholding itself, watching him with some tiny portion of itself. The larger whole understood the universe and could manipulate massive sections of space-time.

"Say nothing to these others." Again the statement was a direct contact that sounded like spoken words.

The dismay that had seized on Cemp in the last few moments was on the level of desperation. He had entered the Silkie stronghold in the belief that his human training and Kibmadine knowledge gave him a temporary advantage over the space Silkies and that if he did not delay, he could win a battle that might resolve the entire threat from these natural Silkies.

Instead, he had come unsuspecting into the lair of a cosmic giant. He thought, appalled, *Here is what has been called "the Power."*

And if the glimpse he had had was real, then it was such a colossal power that all his own ability and strength were as nothing.

He deduced now that this was what had attacked him twice. "Is that true?" he telepathed on the same band as the incoming thoughts had been on.

"Yes. I admit it."

"Why?" Cemp flashed the question. "Why did you do it?"

"So that I would not have to reveal my existence. My fear is always that if other life forms find out about me, they will analyze how to destroy me."

The direction of the alien thought altered. "But now, listen; do as follows. . . ."

The confession had again stirred Cemp's emotions. The hatred that had been aroused in him had a sustained force deriving from the logic-of-levels stimulation —in this instance the body's response to an attempt at total destruction. Therefore, he had difficulty now restraining additional automatic reactions.

But the pieces of the puzzle were falling into place. So, presently he was able, at the request of the monster, to say to E-Lerd and the other Silkies, "You take a while to think this over. And when the Silkies who have defected arrive from Earth, I'll talk to them. We can then have another discussion."

It was such a complete change of attitude that the two Silkies showed their surprise. But he saw that to them the change had the look of weakness and that they were relieved.

"I'll be back here in one hour!" he telepathed to E-Lerd. Whereupon he turned and climbed up and out of the courtyard, darting to an opening that led by a roundabout route deeper into the planetoid.

Again the low, slow vibration touched his receptors. "Come closer!" the creature urged.

Cemp obeyed, on the hard-core principle that either he could defend himself—or he couldn't. Down he went, past a dozen screens, to a barren cave, a chamber that had been carved out of the original meteorite stuff. It was not even lighted. As he entered, the direct thought touched his mind again: "Now we can talk."

Cemp had been thinking at furious speed, striving to

adjust to a danger so tremendous that he had no way of evaluating it. Yet the Power had revealed itself to him rather than let E-Lerd find out anything. That seemed to be his one hold on it; and he had the tense conviction that even that was true only as long as he was inside the planetoid.

He thought, . . . *Take full advantage!*

He telepathed, "After those attacks, you'll have to give me some straight answers, if you expect to deal with me."

"What do you want to know?"

"Who are you? Where do you come from? What do you want?"

It didn't know who it was. "I have a name," it said. "I am the Glis. There used to be many like me long ago. I don't know what happened to them."

"But *what* are you?"

It had no knowledge. An energy life form of unknown origin, traveling from one star system to another, remaining for a while, then leaving.

"But why leave? Why not stay?" sharply.

"The time comes when I have done what I can for a particular system."

By using its enormous power, it transported large ice-and-air meteorites to airless planets and made them habitable, cleared away dangerous space debris, altered poisonous atmospheres into nonpoisonous ones. . . .

"Presently the job is done, and I realize it's time to go on to explore the infinite cosmos. So I make my pretty picture of the inhabited planets, as you saw, and head for outer space."

"And the Silkies?"

They were an old meteorite life form.

"I found them long ago, and because I needed mobile units that could think, I persuaded them into a permanent relationship."

Cemp did not ask what persuasive methods had been

used. In view of the Silkies' ignorance of what they had a relationship with, he divined that a sly method had been used. But still, what he had seen showed an outwardly peaceful arrangement. The Glis had agents— the Silkies—who acted for it in the world of tiny movements. They, in turn, had at their disposal bits and pieces of the Glis's own "body," which could apparently be programmed for specific tasks beyond the Silkies' ability to perform.

"I am willing," said the Glis, "to make the same arrangement with your government for as long as I remain in the solar system."

But absolute secrecy would be necessary.

"Why?"

There was no immediate reply, but the communication band remained open. And along the line of communication there flowed an essence of the reaction from the Glis—an impression of unmatched power, of a being so mighty that all other individuals in the universe were less by some enormous percentage.

Cemp felt staggered anew. But he telepathed, "I must tell someone. Somebody has to know."

"No other Silkies—absolutely."

Cemp didn't argue. All these millennia, the Glis had kept its identity hidden from the space Silkies. He had a total conviction that it would wreck the entire planetoid to prevent them from learning it.

He had been lucky. It had fought him at a level where only a single chamber of the meteorite had been destroyed. It had restricted itself.

"Only the top government leaders and the Silkie Council may know," the Glis continued.

It seemed an adequate concession; yet Cemp had an awful suspicion that in the long past of this creature every person who uncovered its secret had been murdered.

Thinking thus, he could not compromise. He demanded, "Let me have a complete view of you—what I caught a fleeting glimpse of earlier."

He sensed, then, that the Glis hesitated.

Cemp urged, "I promise that only the persons you named will be told about this—but we *must* know!"

Floating there in the cave in his Silkie form, Cemp felt a change of energy tension in the air and in the ground. Although he put forth no additional probing energies, he recognized that barriers were going down. And presently he began to record.

His first impression was of hugeness. Cemp estimated, after a long, measuring look, that the creature, a circular rocklike structure, was about a thousand feet in diameter. It was alive, but it was not a thing of flesh and blood. It "fed" from some inner energy that rivaled what existed in the heart of the sun.

And Cemp noticed a remarkable phenomenon. Magnetic impulses that passed through the creature and impinged on his senses were altered in a fashion that he had never observed before—as if they had passed through atoms of a different structure than anything he knew.

He remembered the fleeting impression he had had from the molecule. This was the same but on a massive scale. What startled him was that all his enormous training in such matters gave no clue to what the structure might be.

"Enough?" asked the creature.

Doubtfully, Cemp said, "Yes."

Glis accepted his reluctant agreement as a complete authorization. What had been a view through and past the cave wall disappeared abruptly.

The alien thought spoke into his mind, "I have done a very dangerous thing for me in thus revealing myself. Therefore, I again earnestly impress on you the importance of a limited number of people being told what you have just witnessed."

In secrecy, it continued, lay the greatest safety, not only for it, but for Cemp.

"I believe," said the creature, "that what I can do is overwhelming. But I could be wrong. What disturbs me is, there is only one of me. I would hate to suddenly feel the kind of fear that might motivate me to destroy an entire system."

The implied threat was as deadly—and as possible—as anything Cemp had ever heard. Cemp hesitated, feeling overwhelmed, desperate for more information.

He flashed, "How old do Silkies get?" and added quickly, "We've had no experience, since none has yet died a natural death."

"About a thousand of your Earth years," was the answer.

"What have you in mind for Earth-born Silkies? Why did you want us to return here?"

Again there was a pause; once more the sense of colossal power. But presently with it there came a reluctant admission that new Silkies, born on planets, normally had less direct knowledge of the Glis than those who had made the latest trip.

Thus, the Glis had a great interest in ensuring that plenty of time was allowed for a good replacement crop of unknowing young Silkies.

It finished, "You and I shall have to make a special agreement. Perhaps you can have E-Lerd's position and be my contact."

Since E-Lerd no longer remembered that he was the contact, Cemp had no sense of having being offered anything but . . . danger.

He thought soberly, *I'll never be permitted to come back here, once I leave.*

But that didn't matter. The important thing was— get away! At once!

# XVIII

AT THE Silkie Authority, the computer gave four answers.

Cemp rejected two of them at once. They were, in the parlance of computer technology, "trials." The machine simply presented all the bits of information, strung out in two lookovers. By this means a living brain could examine the data in segments. But Cemp did not need such data—not now.

Of the remaining two answers, one postulated a being akin to a god. But Cemp had experienced the less-than-godlike powers of the Glis, in that it had twice failed to defeat him. True, he believed that it had failed to destroy him because it did not wish to destroy the planetoid. But an omnipotent god would not have found that a limitation.

He had to act as if the amazing fourth possibility were true. The picture that had come through in that possibility was one of ancientness. The mighty being hidden in the planetoid predated most planetary systems.

"In the time from which it derives," said the computer, "there were, of course, stars and star systems, but they were different. The natural laws were not what they are today. Space and time have made adjustments since then, grown older; therefore, the present appearance of the universe is different from that which the Glis knew at its beginnings. This seems to give it an advantage, for it knows some of the older shapes of atoms and molecules and can re-create them. Certain of these combinations reflect the state of matter when it was—the best comparison—younger."

103

The human government group, to whom Cemp presented these data, was stunned. Like himself, they had been basing their entire plan on working out a compromise with the space Silkies. Now, suddenly, here was a colossal being with unknown power.

"Would you say," asked one man huskily, "that to a degree the Silkies are slaves of this creature?"

Cemp said, "E-Lerd definitely didn't know what he was dealing with. He simply had what he conceived to be a scientific system for utilizing a force of nature. The Glis responded to his manipulation of this system, as if it were simply another form of energy. But I would guess that it controlled him, perhaps through preconditioning installed long ago."

As he pointed out, such a giant life form would not be concerned with the everyday living details of its subjects. It would be satisfied with having a way of invariably getting them to do what it wanted.

"But what *does* it want?" That came from another man.

"It goes around doing good," said Cemp with a tight smile. "That's the public image it tried to give me. I have the impression that it's willing to make over the solar system to our specifications."

At this point Mathews spoke. "Mr. Cemp," he said, "what does all this do to the Silkie situation?"

Cemp said that the Silkies who had defected had clearly acted hastily. "But," he finished, "I should tell you that I find the space Silkies a very likeable group. In my opinion, they are not the problem. They have the same problem, in another way, that we have."

"Nat," said Charley Baxter, "do you trust this monster?"

Cemp hesitated, remembering the deadly attacks, remembering that only the Kibmadine defense screen and energy-reversal process had saved him. He remembered, too, that the great being had been compelled to reveal its presence to prevent him from forcing E-Lerd to open his mind—which would have informed the space Silkies of the nature of the Power.

"No!" he said.

Having spoken, he realized that a simple negative was not answer enough. It could not convey the reality of the terrifying danger that was out there in space.

He said slowly, "I realize that my own motives may be suspect in what I am about to say, but it's my true opinion. I think all Earth Silkies should be given full knowledge of the Kibmadine attack-and-defense system at once and that they should be assigned to work in teams to keep a constant watch on the Glis, permitting no one to leave the planetoid—except to surrender."

There was a pregnant silence. Then a scientist said in a small voice, "Any chance of logic of levels' applying?"

"I don't see how," said Cemp.

"I don't either," said the man unhappily.

Cemp addressed the group again. "I believe we should gird ourselves to drive this thing from the solar system. We're not safe until it's gone."

As he finished speaking, he sensed an energy tension . . . familiar! He had a sensation, then, of cosmic distance and cosmic time—opening. Power unlimited!

It was the same feeling he had had in the second attack, when his senses had been confused.

The fear that came to Cemp in that moment had no parallel in his experience. It was the fear of a man who suddenly has a fleeting glimpse of death and destruction for all his own kind and for his planet.

As he had that awful consciousness, Cemp whirled from where he was standing. He ran headlong toward the great window behind him, shattering it with an arc of lightning as he did so. And with eyes closed against the flying glass, he plunged out into the empty air seventy stories above the ground.

As he fell, the fabric of space and time collapsed

around him like a house of cards tumbling. Cemp transformed into class-C Silkie and became immensely more perceptive. Now he sensed the nature of the colossal energy at work—a gravitational field so intense that it actually closed in upon itself. Encompassing all things, organic and inorganic, it squeezed with irresistible power. . . .

Defensively, Cemp put up, first, his inverter system . . . and perceived that that was not the answer.

Instantly, he triggered gravity transformation—an infinitely variable system that converted the encroaching superfield to a harmless energy in relation to himself.

With that, he felt the change slow. It did not stop. He was no longer so involved, so enveloped; yet he was not completely free.

He realized what held him. He was oriented to this massive segment of space-time. To an extent, anything that happened here happened to him. To that extent, he could not get away.

The world grew dim. The sun disappeared.

Cemp saw with a start that he was inside a chamber and realized that his automatic screens had protected him from striking the hard, glittering walls.

And he became aware of three other realities. The chamber was familiar, in that there below him was one of the glowing images of a planet. The image showed the oceans and the continents, and since he was looking down at it, he felt that he was somehow back inside the Silkie planetoid, in one of the "art" rooms.

What was different was that as he looked down at the planetary image, he saw the familiar outlines of the continents and oceans of Earth. And he realized that the feeling of a virtually unlimited force pressing in was a true explanation of what was happening.

The ancient monster that lived at the core of the planetoid had taken Earth, compressed it and everything on it from an 8,000-mile-in-diameter planet into a hundred-foot ball, and added the ball to its fabulous collection.

It was not a jewel-like image of Earth there in the floor—it was Earth itself.

Even as he had the thought, Cemp sensed that the planetoid was increasing its speed.

He thought, *We're leaving the solar system.*

In a matter of minutes, as he hovered there, helpless to act, the speed of the planetoid became hundreds, then thousands of miles a second.

After about an hour of continuing acceleration, the velocity of the tiny planetoid, in its ever-widening hyperbolic orbit, was nearly half that of light.

A few hours later, the planetoid was beyond the orbit of Pluto, and it was traveling at near light speed.

And still accelerating . . .

# XIX

CEMP BEGAN to brace himself. Anger spilled through him like a torrent down a rocky decline.

"You incredible monster!" he telepathed.

No answer.

Cemp raged on, "You're the most vicious creature that ever existed. I'm going to see that you get what's coming to you!"

This time he got a reply. "I'm leaving the solar system forever," said the Glis. "Why don't you get off before it's too late? I'll let you get away."

Cemp had no doubt of that. He was its most dangerous enemy, and his escape and unexpected appearance must have come as a hideous shock to the Glis.

"I'm not leaving," he retorted, "until you undo what you've done to Earth."

There was silence.

"Can you and will you?" Cemp demanded.

"No. It's impossible." The response came reluctantly. "But you could, if you wanted to, bring Earth back to size."

"No. But I now wish I had not taken your planet," said the Glis unhappily. "It has been my policy to leave alone inhabited worlds that are protected by powerful life forms. I simply could not bring myself to believe that any Silkie was really dangerous to me. I was mistaken."

It was not the kind of repentance that Cemp respected. "Why can't you . . . unsqueeze it?" he persisted.

It seemed that the Glis could create a gravity field, but it could not reverse such a field. It said apologetically, "It would take as much power to undo it as it took to do it. Where is there such power?"

Where, indeed? But still he could not give up. "I'll teach you what antigravity is like," Cemp offered, "from what I can do in my own energy-control system."

But the Glis pointed out that it had had the opportunity to study such systems in other Silkies. "Don't think I didn't try. Evidently antigravity is a late manifestation of matter and energy. And I'm an early form —as you, and only you, know."

Cemp's hope faded suddenly. Somehow, he had kept believing that there was a possibility. There wasn't.

The first grief touched him, the first real acceptance of the end of Earth.

The Glis was communicating again. "I can see that you and I now have a serious situation between us. So we must arrive at an agreement. I'll make you the leader of the Silkie nation. I'll subtly influence everything and everyone to fit your wishes. Women—as many as you desire. Control—as much as you want. Future actions of the planetoid, you and I shall decide."

Cemp did not even consider the offer. He said grimly, "You and I don't think alike. I can just imagine trusting you to leave me alone if I ever took the chance of changing to human form." He broke off, then said curtly, "The deal as I see it is a limited truce while I consider what I can do against you and you figure out what you can do to me."

"Since that's the way you feel," was the harsh reply, "let me make my position clear. If you begin any action against me, I shall first destroy Earth and the Silkie nation and then give you my attention."

Cemp replied in his own steely fashion, "If you ever damage anything I value—and that includes all Silkies and what's left of Earth—I'll attack you with everything I've got."

The Glis said scornfully, "You have nothing that can touch me—except those defense screens that reverse the attack flow. That way, you can use my own force against me. So I won't attack. Therefore—permanent stalemate."

Cemp said, "We'll see."

The Glis said, "You yourself stated that your levels of logic wouldn't work on me."

"I meant not directly," said Cemp. "There are many indirect approaches to the mind."

"I don't see how anything like that can work on me," was the reply.

At that moment, Cemp didn't either.

## XX

THROUGH MILES of passageways, up as well as down and roundabout, Cemp made his way. The journey took him through long chambers filled with furniture and art objects from other planets.

En route he saw strange and wonderful scenes in bas-relief and brilliant color on one wall after another. And always there were the planets themselves, glowingly beautiful, but horrifying too, in his awareness that each one represented a hideous crime.

His destination was the city of the Silkies. He followed the internal pathway to it because he dared not leave the planetoid to take an external route. The Glis had virtually admitted that it had not anticipated that he, its most dangerous enemy, would survive. So if he ever left these caves, he would have no further choice, no chance to decide on what the penalty—if any—or the outcome should be and no part at all in the Silkie future. For he would surely never be allowed to return.

Not that there was any purpose in him—his grief was too deep and terrible. He had failed to protect, failed to realize, failed in his duty.

Earth was lost. It was lost quickly, completely, a disaster so great that it could not even be contemplated for more than instants at a time.

At intervals, he mourned Joanne and Charley Baxter and other friends among the Special People and the human race.

By the time he was sunk into these miseries, he had taken up an observation position on top of a tree overlooking the main street of the Silkie city. There he waited, with all his signal systems constantly at peak alert.

While he maintained his tireless vigil, the life of the Silkie community had its being around him. The Silkies continued to live mostly as humans, and this began to seem significant.

Cemp thought, shocked, *They're being kept vulnerable!*

In human form, they could all be killed in a single flash of intolerable flame.

He telepathed on the Glis band, "Free them from that compulsion or I'll tell them the truth about what you are."

An immediate, ferocious answer came: "You say one word, and I shall wipe out the entire nest."

Cemp commanded, "Release them from that compulsion, or we come to our crisis right now."

His statement must have given the Glis pause, for there was a brief silence. Then, "I'll release half of them. No more. I must retain some hold over you."

Cemp considered that and realized its truth. "But it has to be on an alternating basis. Half are free for twelve hours, then the other half."

The Glis accepted the compromise without further argument. Clearly, it was prepared to recognize the balance of power.

"Where are we heading?" asked Cemp.

"To another star system."

The answer did not satisfy Cemp. Surely the Glis didn't expect to go on with its malignant game of collecting inhabited planets.

He challenged, "I feel that you have some secret purpose."

"Don't be ridiculous, and don't bother me any more."

Stalemate.

As the days and the weeks went by, Cemp tried to keep track of the distance the planetoid was covering and the direction it was going. The speed of the meteorite had reached nearly a light-year per day, Earth time.

Eighty-two of those days passed. And then there was the feel of slowing down. The deceleration continued all that day and the next. And for Cemp, there was finally no question—he could not permit this strange craft which was now his home to arrive at a destination about which he knew nothing.

"Stop this ship!" he ordered.

The Glis replied angrily, "You can't expect to control such minor things as this!"

Since it could be a deadly dangerous scheme, Cemp replied, "Then open yourself to me. Show me everything you know about this system."

"I've never been here before."

"All right, then that's what I'll see when you open up."

"I can't possibly let you look inside me. You may see something this time that will make me vulnerable to your techniques."

"Then change course."

"No. That would mean I can't go anywhere until you die about a thousand years from now. I refuse to accept such a limitation."

The second reference to Silkie age gave Cemp great pause. On Earth no one had known how long Silkies could live, since none born there had died a natural death. He himself was only thirty-eight years of age.

"Look," he said finally, "if I have only a thousand years, why don't you just sit me out? That must be only a pinpoint in time compared with your lifespan."

"All right, we'll do that!" replied the Glis. But the deceleration continued.

Cemp telepathed, "If you don't turn aside, I must take action."

"What can you do?" was the contemptuous response. It was a good question. What, indeed?

113

"I warn you," said Cemp.

"Just don't tell anyone about me. Other than that, do anything you please."

Cemp said, "I gather you've decided I'm not dangerous. And this is the way you act with those you consider harmless."

The Glis said that had Cemp been able to do something, he would already have done it. It finished, "And so I tell you flatly, I'm going to do as I please; and the only restriction on you is, don't violate my need for secrecy. Now, don't bother me again."

The meaning of the dismissal was clear. He had been judged helpless, categorized as someone whose desires need not be considered. The eighty days of inaction had stood against him. He hadn't attacked; therefore, he couldn't. That was palpably the other's logic.

Well . . . what could he do?

He could make an energy assault. But that would take time to mount, and he could expect that the Silkie nation would be wiped out in retaliation and Earth destroyed.

Cemp decided that he was not ready to force such a calamity.

He was presently dismayed to realize that the Glis's analysis was correct. He could keep his mind shut and respect its need for secrecy—and nothing more.

He ought, it seemed to him, to point out to the Glis that there were different types of secrecy. Gradations. Secrecy about itself was one type. But secrecy about the star system ahead was quite another. The whole subject of secrecy—

Cemp's mind poised. Then he thought, *How could I have missed it?*

Yet, even as he wondered, he realized how it had happened. The Glis's need to withhold knowledge of itself had seemed understandable, and somehow the

114

naturalness of it had made him bypass its implications. But now . . .

*Secrecy,* he thought. *Of course! That's it!*

To Silkies, secrecy was an understood phenomenon.

After a few more seconds of thinking about it, Cemp took his first action. He reversed gravity in relation to the planetoid mass below him. Light as a thistledown, he floated up and away from the treetop that had been his observation post for so long. Soon he was speeding along granite corridors.

## XXI

WITHOUT INCIDENT, Cemp reached the chamber containing Earth.

As he set his signals so that all his screens would protect that precious round ball, Cemp permitted himself another increment of hope.

Secrets! he thought again, and his mind soared.

Life, in its natural impulse, had no secrets.

Baby gurgled or cried or manifested needs instant by instant as each feeling was experienced. But the child, growing older, was progressively admonished and inhibited, subjected to a thousand restraints. Yet all his life the growing being would want openness and unrestraint, would struggle to free himself from childhood conditioning.

Conditioning was not of itself logic of levels, but it was related—a step lower. The appearance was of a control center; that is, a rigidity. But it was a created center and could be repeatedly mobilized by the correct stimulus. That part was automatic.

The decisive fact was that, since the Glis had conditioned itself to secrecy—it was conditionable.

Having reached this penultimate point in his analysis, Cemp hesitated. As a Silkie, he was conditioned to incapacitate rather than kill, to negotiate rather than incapacitate, and to promote well-being everywhere.

Even for the Glis, death should be the final consideration, not the first.

So he telepathed, "In all your long span, you have feared that someone would one day learn how to destroy you. I have to tell you that I am that feared person. So unless you are prepared to back down from those insolent statements of a little while ago, you must die."

The answer came coldly. "I let you go to your planet Earth because I have the real hostages under my complete control—the Silkie nation!"

"That is your final statement?" Cemp questioned.

"Yes. Cease these foolish threats. They are beginning to irritate me."

Cemp now said, "I know where you come from, what you are, and what happened to others like you."

Of course, he knew nothing of the kind. But it was the technique. By stating the generalization, he would evoke from the Glis's perception and memory network, first, the truth. Then, like all living things, the Glis would immediately have the automatic impulse to give forth the information as it actually was.

Yet before it could do so, it would exercise the restraint of secrecy. And that would be an exact pattern, a reaffirmation of similar precise restraints in its long, long past. His problem was to utilize it before it destimulated, because as long as it held, it was the equivalent of a logic-of-levels gestalt.

Having, according to the theory, mobilized it, Cemp transmitted the triggering signal.

A startled thought came from the Glis: "What have you done?"

It was Cemp's turn to be sly, covert, scheming. He said, "I had to call to your attention that you had better deal with me."

It was too late for the Glis to help itself, but the pretense—if successful—might save many lives.

"I wish to point out," said the Glis, "that I have not yet damaged anything of value."

Cemp was profoundly relieved to hear the statement. But he had no regrets. With such a creature as this, he could not hope to repeat what he was doing against it. Once the process was started, it was all or nothing.

"What was it you said before about bargaining?" the Glis asked urgently.

Cemp steeled himself against sympathy.

The Glis continued, "I'll give you all my secrets in exchange for your telling me what you're doing to me. I'm experiencing severe internal disturbance, and I don't know why."

Cemp hesitated. It was a tremendous offer. But he divined that once he made such a promise, he would have to keep it.

What had happened was this: As he had hoped, his final signal had triggered the equivalent of a colony gestalt, in this instance the process by which life forms slowly over the millennia adjusted to exterior change.

And the cycle-completing control centers, the growth-change mechanisms in the great being, were stimulated.

Silkies understood the nature of growth, and of change they knew much from their own bodies. But Silkies were late indeed in the scheme of life. In terms of evolution, their cells were as old as the rocks and the planets. The entire history of life's progression was in every cell of a Silkie.

That could not be true of the Glis. It was from an ancient eon, and it had stopped time within itself. Or at least, it had not passed on its seed, which was the way of change through time. In itself, it manifested old, primitive forms. Great forms they were, but the memory in each cell would be limited to what had gone before. Therefore, it couldn't know what, in holding back as it had, it was holding back from.

"I promise not to go on to the Nijjan system," said the Glis. "Observe—I'm already stopping."

Cemp sensed a cessation of the motion of the planetoid, but it seemed a minor act, not meaningful.

He merely noted, in passing, the identity of the star the Glis had named, observing that since it knew the name, it *had* been there before. This seemed to imply that the Glis had a purpose in going there.

It didn't matter; they were turning away from it, would never reach it. If there was a threat there for Cemp or for Silkies, it was now diverted and had been useful only in that it had forced him to action regardless of the consequences.

The Glis's willingness to make amends when it no longer had any choice was merely a sad commentary on its character, but much too late. Many planets too late, Cemp thought.

How many? he wondered. And because he was in the strange emotional condition of someone whose whole thought and effort are concentrated on a single intensely felt purpose, he asked the question aloud automatically, as it came into his mind.

"I don't think I should tell you; you might hold it against me," the Glis replied.

It must have sensed Cemp's adamant state, for it said quickly, "Eighteen hundred and twenty-three."

So many!

The total of them did not shock Cemp—it hurt him. For one of that countless number of unnecessary dead on those planets was Joanne. Another was Charley Baxter.

"Why have you done all this?" Cemp asked. "Why destroy all those planets?"

"They were so beautiful."

True. Cemp had a sudden mental vision of a great planet hanging in space, its atmosphere ballooning up above the oceans and mountains and plains. He had seen that sight often, yet found it always a thing of splendor beyond all the visual delights of the universe.

The feeling passed, for a planet was beautiful when it was brooded over by its parent sun and not as a shrunken museum piece.

The Glis with its planets was like a head hunter of

old. Skillfully, he had murdered each victim. Patiently, he had reduced the head to its small size. Lovingly, he had placed it in his collection.

For the head hunter, each perfect miniature head was a symbol of his manhood. For the Glis, the planets were . . . what?

Cemp couldn't imagine.

But he had delayed long enough. He sensed incipient violence on the communication band. He said hastily, "All right, I agree—as soon as you do what I want, I'll tell you exactly how I'm attacking you."

"What do you want?"

Cemp said, "First, let the other Silkies go outside."

"But you'll do as I've asked?"

"Yes. When you've released them, put me and the Earth outside, safely."

"Then you'll tell me?"

"Yes."

The Glis threatened, "If you don't, I'll smash your little planet. I will not let you or it escape, if you don't tell me."

"I'll tell you."

# XXII

THE METHOD that was used was, the entire section of the planetoid surrounding Cemp simply lifted up and shot off into the sky. Cemp found himself floating in black, empty space, surrounded by meteorite debris.

The Glis's thought came to him, "I have done my part. Now tell me!"

Even as Cemp complied, he began to wonder if he really understood what was happening.

Uneasiness came. In setting in motion a cycle-completion process, he had taken it for granted that Nature would strike a balance. An old life form had somehow been preserved here, and in its body, evolution was now proceeding at lightning speed. Millions of years of change had already been compressed into minutes of time. Since none other of its kind remained alive, he had assumed that the species had long since evolved to . . . what?

What was this creature? A chrysalis? An egg? Would it become a butterfly of space, a great worm, a gigantic bird?

Such possibilities had not occurred to him before. He had thought only of the possibility of extinction. But—it struck him keenly—he hadn't considered seriously enough what extinction might consist of in its end product.

Indeed, he hadn't thought about the existence of an end product.

Unhappily, Cemp remembered what the computer had reported—that the atomic structure of this giant being reflected a younger state of matter.

Could it be that, as the particles "adjusted" and

changed to current norm, energy would be released on a hitherto unknown scale?

Below, a titanic thing happened.

Part of the planetoid lifted, and a solid ball of red-hot matter, at least a mile thick, lifted slowly out of it. As Cemp drew aside to let the improbable thing past him, he saw that an even more unlikely phenomenon was taking place. The "up" speed of the chunk of now white-hot rock and dirt was increasing—and the mass was growing.

It was well past him, and it was at least a hundred miles in diameter. A minute later, it was five hundred miles thick, and it was still expanding, still increasing in speed.

It expanded to a burning, incredible mass.

Suddenly, it was ten thousand miles in diameter and was still going away, still growing.

Cemp sent out a general alarm: "Get away—as fast as you can. Away!"

As he himself fled, using a reversal of the gravity of the monstrous body behind him, he saw that in those few minutes it had grown more than 100,000 miles in diameter.

It was quite pink at this point—strangely, beautifully pink.

The color altered even as he watched, turning faintly yellow. And the body that emitted the beautiful ocher light was now more than 1,000,000 miles in diameter.

As big as Earth's sun.

In minutes more, it grew to the size of a giant blue sun, ten times the diameter of Sol.

It began to turn pink again, and it grew *one hundred times* in ten minutes. Brighter than Mira the Wonderful, bigger than glorious Ras Algethi.

But pink, not red. A deeper pink than before; not red, so definitely not a variable.

All around was the starry universe, bright with unfamiliar objects that glowed near and far—hundreds of them, strung out like a long line of jack-o'-lanterns.

Below was Earth.

Cemp looked at that scene in the heavens and then at the near, familiar planet, and an awful excitement seized him.

He thought, *Is it possible that everything had to grow, that the Glis's change altered this entire area of space-time?*

Old forms could not keep their suppressed state once the supercolossal pink giant completed the growth that had somehow been arrested from time's beginning.

And so the Glis was now a sun in its prime, but with eighteen hundred and twenty-three planets strung out like so many starry brilliants over the whole near sky.

Everywhere he looked were planets so close to him that they looked like moons. He made a quick, anxious calculation and realized with great relief that all those planets were still within the warming area of the monstrous sun that hung out there, half a light-year away.

As Cemp descended, at the top speed his Silkie body could withstand, into the huge atmosphere blanket that surrounded Earth, everything seemed the same—the land, the sea, the cities. . . .

He swooped low over one highway and observed cars going along it.

He headed for the Silkie Authority in a haze of wonder and saw the shattered window from which he had leaped so dramatically—not yet repaired!

When, moments later, he landed among the same group of men who had been there at his departure, he realized there had been some kind of a time stasis, related to size.

For Earth and its people, that eighty days had been . . . eighty seconds.

Afterward, he would hear how people had experienced what seemed like an earthquake, tension in their bodies, momentary sensory blackout, a brief feeling that it was dark. . . .

Now, as he entered, Cemp transformed to human form and said in a piercing voice, "Gentlemen, prepare for the most remarkable piece of information in the history of the universe. That pink sun out there is not the result of an atmospheric distortion.

"And, gentlemen, Earth now has eighteen hundred inhabited sister planets. Let's begin to organize for a fantastic future!"

Later, comfortably back in his Florida home, Cemp said to Joanne, "Now we can see why the Silkie problem didn't have a solution as things stood. For Earth, two thousand of us was saturation. But in this new sun system . . ."

It was no longer a question of what to do with the 6,000 members of the Silkie nation but of how they could get a hundred such groups to cope with the work to be done.

Quickly!

# XXIII

When the Silkie call for help came, Nat Cemp was exploring the planet that had been given the astronomical designation Minus 1109-93.

The 1109th planet farther away than Earth from the new, mighty sun, revolving at an angle of ninety-three degrees in relation to Earth.

It was a temporary nomenclature. No one took the attitude that Earth was the most important planet of the new system.

Not, apparently, that it was going to matter. On the three planets 1107, 1108, and now 1109 that had been assigned to Cemp, there were no detectable inhabitants. He had been skimming for nearly half a day among the strange, slender buildings that reared like stretched lacework toward the sky. And already it was sadly obvious that here, also, the transition period had been too long for life to survive, that perhaps only Earth and a few others already discovered had been able to make the changeover.

The call for help came as Cemp was floating through a vast generator-building complex. Clear and sharp and urgent, he picked it up from the mechanical relay system between 1109 and 1110.

It said, "All Silkies and government agencies: I have just received a [Silkie word] message from Lan Jedd."

The special Silkie word was a thought form used to describe an after-death Silkie communication phenomenon. As a Silkie descended into death, there was a threshold point at which an isolated neural bundle was activated. The bundle was a telepathic sender, and it quite simply transmitted the final living thoughts,

125

perceptions, and feelings of a Silkie who, at the time the message was sent, was already dead.

The name of the dead Silkie, thus relayed, shocked Cemp. For Lann Jedd and he had been as much friends as any two Silkies ever were, or rather ever were allowed to be. Human beings, and particularly the Special People, had always discouraged Silkie-with-Silkie associations.

Lan and he had chosen to explore adjoining sets of planets at this remote end of the system in order to have relatively unmonitored discussions about the increasing severity of the Silkie-human problem.

So, for Cemp, as the message reached him, the shocking thrill-thought came that except for the sender, he was the nearest "help."

He responded at once with, "Nat Cemp coming immediately. Who are you?"

"Ou-Dan! Calling from 1113-86."

The identification of the sender was disturbing. It was a name of the type and style common to meteorite Silkies, whose existence had until less than a year ago been unknown. The presence of such "original" Silkies in this vastly larger sun system was an unknown, unresolved factor, that which Cemp and Lan Jedd had also talked about in great detail.

It was startling to consider that perhaps Ou-Dan had "listened in" to their discussion. But what especially disturbed Cemp was that he had no confidence in the fighting abilities of these newly arrived Silkies. Therefore, for many hours he would be virtually alone against a mysterious, powerful enemy who had already proved himself strong enough to kill a Silkie.

As he had these awarenesses, Cemp was projecting himself out of the building he was in. Moments later he was rising out of the atmosphere by means of his Silkie method of gravitational reversal.

Literally, the planet expelled his body, which, in his

C-Silkie form, was almost bullet-shaped and ten feet long. In this form his was fully able to operate and live in the vacuum of space.

Once away from the planet, Cemp maintained his expulsion momentum and moved through space by cutting off gravity from all objects in space except in the direction he wanted to go. Thus the outer planets drew him, and he "fell" with ever-increasing speed toward his destination, a special "ship."

In spite of his initial acceleration, it was the usual slow journey of a Silkie traveling by himself through space. So it was several anxious hours before he at last saw the ship in the dark space ahead.

The ship was a defensive vessel that had been built as part of a crash program after Earth became part of the new sun system. Built without walls, utilizing weapons built on principles Cemp had learned from the Glis, it and others like it were part of the safety measures set up in conjunction with exploring so many new and unknown planets.

As soon he was securely in control of the ship, Cemp started it toward Ou-Dan, a distance of only four planets, which was no problem at all to the fast ship.

Once underway, Cemp allowed its relay sender to activate again. Thus, he tuned in to communications that were already in progress from more remote points —Silkies speculating telepathically about what had happened.

What a powerful life form that planet which Lan Jedd had been exploring must have . . . if one or even several of them could kill a fully grown Silkie like Lan! That was the general thought. From all over the system converging Silkies readied for a mass battle with a dangerous opponent.

Unfortunately, it would be quite a while before these more distant helpers arrived on the scene. For at least an Earth day, Ou-Dan and Cemp would be the only living beings on or near the scene.

Arriving at ship speed, Cemp learned that the dead Silkie body had been taken by Ou-Dan over to a meteorite that circled 1113-86.

The strange bright-dark of space with its black "sky" and the huge, faraway sun glaring with a thousand reflected brilliances from every rock and metal facet of the meteorite—that was the backdrop.

In such a vast frame, the shattered Silkie body seemed like an atom in infinity. It lay sprawled on a flat spread of rock. In death it bore an even vaguer resemblance to a human being than in life.

There was no indication of how the destruction had been done. Ou-Dan commented telepathically that the body looked collapsed, but it was not much smaller than normal—eight inches at most.

As Cemp gazed silently down at his dead friend, he realized that the worst possible thing had happened. A highly trained adult Silkie, with all that implied in alertness and ability to utilize powerful defensive and offensive energies, had been confronted by another being, and the Silkie had been defeated and killed.

Ou-Dan, looking a little like an elongated meteorite himself, telepathed, "Lan had just reported to me that there were no inhabitants surviving on 1110, 1111, and 1112, and I, working backward, had found the same situation on 1115, 1114, and 1113, when his after-death message came."

A dead Silkie, Cemp thought, and only one clue—that single flash of communication from the mature and powerful Lan Jedd, instants after he died. A mental picture of a pyramidal shape and the thought, *It came from nowhere, from nothingness.*

Cemp felt a chill as he contemplated the fantastic implications of the message. The immense speed of the attack . . . out of nowhere.

Presently, Cemp telepathed to Ou-Dan, "Why don't you come with me, and we'll wait in the ship? Its weapons will help us if we're attacked."

Ou-Dan followed Cemp into an alcove barrier at the heart of the machinery that made up the ship. "But I'm not staying," he said.

Cemp sensed behind the decision, not antagonism, but disinterest.

Ou-Dan's thought came again, "I remained with Lan's dead body out of courtesy till someone arrived. Now that you're here, I plan to return to Earth."

"It's safer in the ship," Cemp urged.

He pointed out that it was an Earth Silkie maxim never to take unnecessary chances. Ou-Dan's plan to go out by himself into space seemed a risk of this kind.

"It would be purely accidental," was the reply, "if I met the killer in these vast reaches. My guess is that he spotted Lan when he used the relay system to communicate with me. So as I see it, the closer you are to a ship, the greater your danger."

The analysis had its own reasonableness. But why, since Ou-Dan had joined the exploration group in the first place, leave now? Cemp asked the question.

Ou-Dan said that because of Cemp's action in saving the meteorite Silkies from the Glis eight months before, Ou-Dan felt obligated to tell him that he considered this to be a crisis. But it was probably typical of the many crises that would occur in the future in a new system comprising eighteen hundred and twenty-three habitable planets. So the time to resolve Silkie rights in relation to human beings was now.

Ou-Dan predicted that the Silkie originals would undoubtedly take no further action until their legal situation with Earth was settled.

"The others and I came out to get the feel of being involved," said Ou-Dan. "So I can tell you right now that we're not going to settle for being police officers like you. And of course, we're not going to give up our ability to change to any form or shape of body.

"After all," Ou-Dan continued tolerantly, "just because you're limited to the Silkie-human cycle doesn't mean we have to be."

They had been talking mentally at the superspeed of thoughts synchronized with magnetic carrier waves. It would have actually required a small book for a transcript of the details of their messages to each other; the overtones were that numerous.

Now, for the period required for a private thought, Cemp put up a barrier. The fantastic subject of change of form was not one he was prepared to discuss with anyone. In fact, he had instructions from the Silkie Authority to keep secret his special knowledge.

The original Silkies—like Ou-Dan—had a basic ability to change into any living shape or form that could contain, expand, or compress the total number of molecules involved; not merely a human form. Theirs was, however, an elementary-level transformation, beginning with a general internal and external resemblance—not very refined but adequate for any reasonable purpose. In addition, in the presence of a life form, they could, by a continuous rapid scanning-and-feedback method, duplicate that life form at virtually any level of refinement—as long as the being who was duplicated was close by.

Earth Silkies, on the other hand, had been biologically limited to the human—Silkie B—Silkie C change, which was automatic once it was set in motion.

Only Nat Cemp, of the Earth Silkies, could go beyond the Silkie-human cycle.

In confronting the remarkable Kibmadine, he had learned its perfect method of metamorphic ability. He needed only the memory of someone once met, and he could become that person or being with total duplication.

Having had these thoughts and hidden them, Cemp

telepathed in a temporizing way, "Don't underestimate human beings."

"I won't," retorted Ou-Dan, "so long as they have you fooled into being on their side."

Cemp said, "Even with the 6,000 original Silkies added to our own numbers, the total Silkie population of the entire universe is less than 8,000. Such a minority has to adjust to the vast planetary populations of other life forms."

Ou-Dan said, "I don't have to adjust to anything. I'm free to do as I please."

Cemp said, "All through human history, wherever people got the right to make their own choices, they presently refused to cooperate even for the common good. Soon, each person set himself up as having an opinion as good as that of anyone else. Naturally, they soon fell under the influence of individuals with skillful systems, and in the end were maneuvered into a new slavery. Now, here you are making the same error of refusing to cooperate."

"Let others cooperate with us," was the reply. "We're the superior beings."

"If we were so great," Cemp flashed back, "how come there are so few of us left?"

"Well . . ." Ou-Dan was impatient. "We were unlucky that we ran into a race with even more capability than we had. At least, that's the legend. And of course, after that we were in that meteorite under the control of the Glis, and our numbers were kept limited."

Cemp pointed out gently that control of Silkies by the Glis was the slave condition. "Therefore," he said, "we may deduce that long ago, Silkies reached the state of refusing to cooperate for the common good. We can picture enormous, vaulting egos, opinionated and ridiculous, never once having a true survival thought.

"We can," Cemp continued, "picture Silkies refusing to abide by any system of law, going out into space if anyone threatened them, feeling absolutely impregnable. And then, one day out there in the dark reaches, they met their match and were hunted down individually by a remorseless enemy."

"I don't see how we free Silkies can even talk to someone as conformist as you are," said Ou-Dan.

"Reliable is the word," answered Cemp. "I can be trusted to do what I say. Evidently, you and your originals cannot even decide what role you want to play."

"Why should we have a role? Why should we work at all, at anything? Why shouldn't human beings work for us instead of we for them? That's a perfectly fair question."

Cemp explained that human beings seemed to be easily surviving their present association with Silkies. But this might not be true if the conditions of association were altered.

Ou-Dan seemed indifferent to the possibility. And Cemp realized it was a lot to expect that someone who had had no previous contact with human beings would care about them. But Cemp, who had been born to a human mother, did care. So he said, with the intent of ending the discussion, "We'll have a general meeting soon. We'll talk then."

Such a meeting had already been proposed by Charley Baxter, head of the Silkie Authority. Baxter was as anxious about the attitude of the original Silkies as Cemp was.

Ou-Dan accepted the end of conversation with, "I have nothing more to learn here. Goodbye." Whereupon he launched into space and was quickly lost from view. Presently, he did not even register on the magnetic band as any different from the meteorite flotsam and jetsam that populated all areas of space.

# XXIV

IN THIS distant point in space, with all the trigger systems for the "ship" set for instant reaction, Cemp waited for he knew not what.

The open-to-space ship was itself lightless. Artificial light on any level interfered with the sensitive instruments that monitored the protective weaponry. It was enough problem for the equipment around him that he himself had to be taken account of.

Periodically, Cemp made a complete check of that equipment, establishing each time that every relay was ready to snap and that each device was separately set to permit the presence of his Silkie shape and mass and of that portion of his life energy which he could not contain within himself.

While he waited, Cemp gazed "down" in the general direction of Earth. The view below had the forever-new quality of light and form that had passed a threshold point of abundance. There were many, many brilliant planetary lights in the dark sky of Earth's new super-sun system, and the sheer number of planets, each with a different coloration, made for a timelessly beautiful panorama.

For Cemp, it *was* below and down because he had long ago oriented himself in such human terms. In his Silkie body he always operated at what would have been face down in a human being. So he had a right and a left, a front and a back, and an up and a down.

In the several conversations that he conducted with far Earth, Cemp could obtain no additional advice about any other precautions he might take. No one believed that any living being could approach him unnoticed out there at the remote edge of the system.

Yet Lan Jedd's "report" indicated that there would be no advance warning.

There wasn't.

At the moment of the attack, Cemp had waited in the ship exactly four hours, eighteen minutes, and forty-two seconds, Earth time.

The being who for a few split instants was exposed to Cemp's perception had the shape of an inverted pyramid. It was interesting that in the transmission of the same image from the now deceased Lan Jedd, the inversion had not come through. The transmitting computer, consulting its analogs, had produced a pyramid stereotype wherein the base was down and the point up.

In fact, the base was up and the point down.

That was all Cemp had time to "see," for the creature was in the trap only momentarily. A less speedy perception than that of a Silkie would have noticed at best a shadow darken a lighted space.

Despite the colossal speed of the being's withdrawal, Cemp, with his heightened Silkie perception, was able to examine awareness centered in himself that had automatically recorded more data. Thus Cemp continued to view where it had been through a series of neural and energy receptors that played back their information for his evaluation.

He realized, fascinated, that during the moment it was in the trap, the creature had attacked and tried to kill him. But he had been saved by the defenses of the trap.

A strong impulse came to study the battle, to discover immediately what had made him vulnerable, why his own screens wouldn't have worked.

Cemp fought that impulse, thinking, *Put the battle aside. Examine it last.*

For an attack was only that—energy, force, whatever. It was the being's method of approaching the trap that everybody down the line wanted to know about—where *had* the fantastic thing come from?

Studying the afterimages, Cemp saw with amazement that the pyramid shape was actually an energy projection from a source. He could not get a good look at the being at the source, it withdrew so rapidly.

Considering the incredible speed of that withdrawal, he recalled a scientifically oriented speculative discussion he had had with other Silkies about his encounter with the Glis. Now, he felt that Glis experience again in his mind—and that wasn't it.

The discovery appalled him, for what he had perceived had been something; and then it was nothing. Something to nothing. Nothing to something to nothing. What could it be?

Cemp had one receptor that had on it a vague perception—so vague that it gained reality only because he played it for himself a dozen times. Even then it remained unclear. But with so many replays he had an impression, if such it could be called, that the energy point that was the apparent source of the inverted pyramid had another point at some vast distance beyond it. And behind—beyond—that point was still another point and beyond that another and more points in the vaster distance . . . Or was it distance? Cemp couldn't decide.

After viewing and re-viewing the impression, so shadowy and uncertain, he consciously compared what he saw to an endless image reflected in two perfect mirrors facing each other.

But even that was only an analogy, because the images extended into only one mirror and not the other. It was a unidirectional phenomenon.

It was a mystery he could not solve, so he uneasily turned his attention to the life-and-death battle he had fought.

Like the other aspects of that momentary contact, the engagement could be studied only in the confusing aftermath. Examined thus, it proved to have started the split instant the creature arrived. The trap, consisting in its first phase of a Glis-type molecule with the gravity power of a planet, had instantaneously oriented itself to the enemy. It *was* instantaneous because, of course, gravity has no lag; there is no moment of waiting while it goes through a process of adjustment.

The molecule, that remarkable discovery of the ancient nature of matter the secret of which Cemp had got from the Glis, reached with the power of an entire world—and attached itself to the alien. Hindered him.

The attacker, thus handicapped, nevertheless did something—what, Cemp had no idea. All Cemp's great defenses were up—his energy screens, his magnetic methods of turning aside radiation, what he had learned from the Kibmadine about using attack energy against the attacker. . . .

The attack was not on an energy band. Cemp's defenses had no effect on it. He had felt a change in his whole body, a sudden sense of inward-collapsing distortion. . . .

His thoughts had twisted strangely. Unable to put up a single barrier, Cemp had felt himself spin toward death—

The next second, the creature, hindered by the molecule, disappeared.

And the battle was over.

## XXV

URGENTLY, Cemp opened a line to Earth. He was quickly deluged with questions.

And someone had had the same thought he had had —that the pyramid was a weapon operating through some mirror principle from an actual distance. Thus, it was argued, the effect of nothing to something to nothing was like a mirror being turned on and off in the time it took to operate a push-pull switch.

"No!" answered Cemp. "It was a life form. I sensed its aliveness."

That ended that part of the argument.

Charley Baxter came on. "Your data are being fed into the computer, Nat," he said gravely. "While we wait, would you like to speak to your wife?"

"Of course."

Joanne's thought, when it came through, reflected irritation. "Everybody's so damned secretive about what you're doing," she began.

So they hadn't told her his danger. Cemp was relieved.

"Look," he telepathed, "we're exploring out here and testing a new ship. That's all I'm allowed to say."

It was a truth of sorts. He added, "What have you been up to?"

His attempt at diverting her was successful. Joanne became indignant. "I have had the most horrible experience," she reported.

What she told him was that Silkie women—members of the original Silkies—had called on the human wives of Earth Silkies and urged them to divorce their Silkie husbands. Such a Silkie woman had called on Joanne and demanded that she divorce Cemp.

The Silkie woman had pointed out bluntly that Cemp as a Silkie would live to be at least a thousand years old. And of course, Joanne was more mortal than that by far.

"So," the Silkie woman had urged, "why not face the reality of that now?"

. . . While Joanne was still young.

Cemp had the unhappy feeling that the problem was more severe than Joanne knew. A thousand years was as long as the Glis, for its own reasons, had allowed meteorite Silkies to live. What a Silkie's actual life span was, no one knew.

Yet he had always felt that these matters would be resolved in their own good time. Joanne was under thirty. Her present life expectancy was about one hundred and fifty. Long before she reached that age, human immortality might become possible.

Questioning her, he discovered that Joanne had toughly pointed out all these things to the Silkie woman and had given as much as she received.

It was not a moment for Cemp to consider what changes might come in the Silkie-human tangle. He telepathed with warmth, "Don't worry about any of this. You're my darling."

"That's a powerful point," said Joanne sweetly, "but don't think you've fooled me for a moment. I sense there's a big event coming up in your life, and you're taking it in stride as usual."

"Well—" Cemp began.

"It's really an unresolvable dilemma," answered Joanne.

"What is?" Cemp asked in surprise. He quickly realized that Joanne's concern was not with the danger but, of all things, with his lack of fear.

She said almost tearfully, "If you feel so confident against such a mighty enemy—what's going to become of Silkie-human relations?"

"Meaning, I presume," said Cemp, "that Silkies don't need humans any more?"

"Well, do they?"

Cemp explained patiently, "In the first place, my confidence is in logic of levels and not in myself."

Joanne brushed that aside. "It's the same thing. Logic of levels is a tool that you can use whether you're associated with humans or not."

"In the second place," Cemp replied, "I don't even know yet whether I'm going to dare use it, though I'm certainly going to threaten it."

"You'll be forced to, and then you'll win, and there you'll be at an incredible height of power and ability."

"In the third place," Cemp continued, "the association between Silkies and humans exists, and I'm particularly happy with what I got out of the transaction—meaning you. Do I seem any smarter?"

"N-no."

"IQ, human-level, eh, still?"

"I suppose so." Reluctant admission.

"I still seem to reason like a human being, correct?"

"But you're so powerful."

"Perhaps you should think of me as a battleship commander," said Cemp. "In this instance, the battleship is my Silkie body, and you're the commander's beloved wife."

The comparison seemed to buoy her, for her mind smiled at him, and she said, "They're motioning me to stop, and I still love you, but goodbye, my dear."

Her communication ceased abruptly.

Charley Baxter came on. "The computer," he said, and there was concern in his thought, "was reminded by your data of something you reported months ago— something the Glis told you during its death throes."

. . . The Glis, realizing that Cemp was a dangerous Silkie, had headed toward a remote star system. This system, according to what the Glis had told Cemp in its final, desperate effort to save itself, was inhabited by an ancient enemy of the Silkies.

These beings called themselves Nijjans, which was a race name with a mighty meaning—Creators of Universes. Or in its fullest sense, The People Who Know the Nature of Things and Can Create Universes at Will.

As Cemp uneasily pondered the hideous possibilities if the analysis was true, Baxter continued in an argumentative overtone, "Nat, the Glis *was* going somewhere. You did get alarmed and you threatened him. As you described it, the Glis stopped and tried to make his peace with you. So whatever system he was pointing toward must be out there in the direction he was going, not too far away."

Since astronomers had got a line on Sol, Earth's former sun, they had already projected a line fairly straight at the Glis's original destination somewhere in near space.

"And," said Baxter, "the system is out there about six light-years beyond you, Nat."

Such details were, of course, of interest. But Cemp was under too much threat for anything but the absolutely decisive points to matter to him.

He telepathed hastily, "Does the computer have any idea how the Nijjan killed Lan or how I should handle him if he comes back with reinforcements?"

Baxter's disturbed reply came, "Nat, this is a terrible thing to tell someone in your situation. But the computer hasn't the faintest idea how the thing came out of nothingness or what the force used against Lan and you was. It says it has no programming that fits and—"

That was all Cemp had time to receive.

At that nanosecond the perceptors that he had projected beyond the Nijjan's first relay point were triggered.

Since he had a communication line open to Earth,

he allowed his recording of danger to go through him and along that line.

The essential of the communication that he thus instantly passed along was, "The Nijjan is back . . . before I'm ready." It seemed like long, long *before*.

There the creature was, in much the same position as the first time, partly inside the ship, a hundred feet away.

But alone! That was the one hopeful aspect.

The inverted pyramidal projection glimmered with flickering energy pulsations.

Cemp now saw that the actual being at the source of the projection was also an inverted pyramid—but in a way only. The base part was much narrower. And it had, he observed, arms and legs. It was about six feet long, and it was beautiful in that its hard, bright skin glittered and shone with changing color.

At the instant of the alien's arrival, the Glis molecule tried to attach itself. But the Nijjan was evidently prepared, for he balanced himself against it somehow and thereafter ignored the molecule.

Cemp grew aware that the creature was looking at him intently from one or more of the bright points at the upper part of its body. Tentatively, Cemp sent a thought on a magnetic wave.

The answer came at once on the same wavelength, came with multiples more force than Cemp was accustomed to receiving. Yet he had his own neural transformers, which stepped the power down to his level. And he had his first communication.

The creature began, "Let's have a conversation."

"You have a lot to explain," Cemp thought back grimly.

"We're puzzled," was the reply. "Suddenly, a nova-sized sun appears only a few light-years from our own system. On investigation, we discover that the system that has so suddenly come into being is the largest planetary family, possibly, in the galaxy. Only a few

141

of the planets are inhabited, but many have been in the past and are no longer so. Climactically, one of our exploring units meets a Silkie, a powerful being known from our antiquity as an enemy. He naturally destroys this being."

"We shall require," said Cemp, "your people to execute this explorer who so instantly—and naturally—took it upon himself to destroy a Silkie."

"It was an ancient reflex, which has now been modified," was the reply. "So execution will not occur. It could have happened to any Nijjan."

"Did you do it?" Cemp asked. "Are you this—what did you call him?—exploring unit?"

"Would it matter?"

"Probably not."

The Nijjan changed the subject. "What do you Silkies do in relation to human beings? What is your role?"

"We're police."

"Oh! That's interesting."

Cemp couldn't see how, and besides, his attention was still concentrated on the other's explanation for the killing of Lan Jedd. He admitted reluctantly to himself that if an attack reflex had indeed been set up long ago in all these creatures and never canceled, it would be difficult to adjudicate intentional murder.

But his next communication acknowledged none of this as he continued, "All right, so here we are, accidentally doomed to occupy a space only a few light-years from each other. And we have eighteen hundred habitable planets. How many do you have?"

"That's a difficult question to answer. We don't think in terms of having a planet of our own. But I sense this is a difficult concept for you, so I'll say we probably do own one planet—our original home."

"Do you want any more?"

"Not in the sense that you mean. All this is too new. But our basic purposes are peaceful."

Cemp didn't believe him.

It should have been true. The passing of the eons should have ended old impulses of hatred and destruction. On Earth, a thousand descendants of enemies of an equal number of yesteryears now lived side by side, at peace apparently forever.

Of course, this was not quite the same. The Nijjans were not descendants. They were the same beings who, long ago indeed, had attained the heights of their civilization and immortality. These were the same creatures who had in the distant past hated and sought to exterminate the Silkies—so the Glis had told Cemp.

In that olden time, desiring to have the Silkies as servants, the mighty Glis had offered them a symbiotic relationship as the price for saving them—and the Silkies had accepted.

But that, with the transformation and defeat of the Glis, was now over. And the Silkies were again on their own. They could expect no help from any outside source.

It was a shaking thought, but Cemp was unrelenting. "I can't accept your disclaimer," he said, "because why, when you first arrived here, presumably with your attack reflex already canceled, did you try to kill me?"

The Nijjan's reply was, "It was a defensive act. Something grabbed me. I see now that it is an unusual gravitational manifestation. But in that first moment I reacted in two ways—immediate counterattack and retreat. As soon as I had considered what the threat was, I decided to return. And here I am. So let's talk."

It was a good explanation; yet Cemp's feeling remained—he didn't believe the story, couldn't accept it, considered it motivated by the Nijjan's desire to gain time. He had a desperate conviction that his danger was increasing with each passing moment.

Cemp wondered, *What does he want the time for?*

The obvious answer was time to explore the ship, of course. Its structure, its weaponry.

"If what you say is true," Cemp countered, "then you will tell me what your method of attack was. How did your colleague kill a Silkie?"

"It would be foolish of me to reveal my advantages," answered the Nijjan. "How do I know what *your* plans are?"

Though that, also, was basically true, it was a total stop. Yet there were still things he could learn.

Cemp sent out magnetic waves on all bands, designed to stir reactions in the other's body. He recorded the information that came back on magnetic waves passing through the Nijjan's body at the time his messages arrived.

He used radar and read the data that bounced back. And geon waves, those strange time-delay patterns.

He used the Ylem energy also—and that was dangerously close to being a weapon. But his purpose, which he telepathed to the Nijjan, was to elicit a reaction.

If there was, in fact, any understanding for him in the waves and energies that reflected or came back to him, Cemp could not analyze it.

With an effort, Cemp braced himself against the failure and commanded, "Leave! Unless you reveal the method of murder, I refuse to continue this conversation. And I assure you that no further negotiations between our two groups can occur until that revelation is made."

The Nijjan answered, "I cannot give such data without authorization. So why not come with me and talk to . . ." He used a mental meaning that implied a government but had a different implication, which Cemp could not evaluate.

Cemp answered, "That would place me at your mercy."

"Somebody has to negotiate. Why not you?"

One thing, it seemed to Cemp, could be said for this Nijjan. As a deceiver, if that was what he was, he was certainly consistent.

Telepathically, he temporized, "How would I go with you?"

"Move past me, across and into the projection of myself at a distance of . . ." The Nijjan named a measurement in terms of a certain magnetic wavelength.

Once more, Cemp felt grudging admiration for this being. He thought, *For all I know, if I do that, that will be his method of killing me.*

What was fascinating was that he was being maneuvered into doing it to himself.

The extreme skillfulness of the deception involved, in this near-ultimate moment, focused Cemp's attention on *that* aspect.

As he realized the possibility, Cemp did two things. He sent a beam to the trap mechanism that controlled the molecule with its planet-sized gravity, and he released the molecule's hold on the Nijjan.

The rationale of this first action was that the being must be bracing himself against that gravity; he must be using power to hold himself away from it. At the moment of release, he would have to deal with the resultant inertia, the equivalent of a planet's centrifugal thrust.

The second thing Cemp did was more subtle, but he did it at the same instant. He tried logic of levels on the one behavior that he had now belatedly noticed in the Nijjan.

And because he wasn't sure it would work and didn't want to give away what, until now, had been a human-Silkie secret, he hoped the gravity release would confuse the great being who had come into this trap with such total confidence in his own ability against Silkies. He hoped it would confuse the Nijjan, render him momentarily vulnerable, and, somehow, prevent disaster.

The behavior Cemp believed he had observed was—the creature was manifesting the famous betrayal pattern.

From the point of view of logic of levels, it was a minor event in the brain. Since it was the basic winning cycle of life, nothing decisive could be done against it. By triggering it, he could force the Nijjan to win more—which was ironic and could lead to unknown consequences. But it was the only opening available.

Three things happened at the same moment. The molecule released; the betrayal cycle triggered; and Cemp entered the path of the energy beam that created the larger pyramid.

He felt a sensation different from anything he had ever experienced. Under him and around him, the trap-ship . . . vanished.

He perceived that he was in a strange . . . not place, for there was nothing. But . . . what?

# XXVI

IN A GROUP, only the leader can betray. And he must betray, or be ready to betray, or there is no group.

Everyone else has to conform, fit in, follow the rules, be a supporter without qualifications; even to think an objection is wrong.

You must swear fealty to the leader "without mental reservations." You must support the code and, ideally, report to the leader's police any deviations from it on the part of others and on the part of yourself.

At any moment for the good of the group—by the leader's judgment alone—you can be betrayed (sacrificed) without any other explanation being required.

Periodically, you or some other conformist must be betrayed as a matter of policy, even if you have not deviated from the code by any previously applied standard of judgment.

The leader's act of betraying you of itself makes you guilty. Immediately every other person in the group must disconnect from you without mental reservations.

The rule of betrayal by the leader alone applies under any group system, including the elective—where the leader's immediate aides are his group.

As a group grows larger, the leader delegates his betrayal rights to unevenly qualified persons who act in his name. Where this process of delegation continues and expands, there are alleviations because not every subleader is as sensitive to the danger of nonconformism as the leader is.

But the leader who can read minds and who utilizes the betrayal cycle through a remorseless police-control method can remain leader . . . forever.

Thus, betrayal, consistently applied, wins at all levels; and the highest level is . . .

For Cemp, a combination event was occurring. He felt as if someone with whom he was in a kind of total telepathic communication was small. *So* small. Or—a sudden puzzlement struck him—was he, in fact, very large? Incredibly large—larger than the universe? . . . The being whose thoughts Cemp was receiving rejected the concept of vastness. It was more comfortable to feel . . . small.

Satisfied that he was a mere point, the being considered what he might *become*. He thought, and Cemp received the thought along with the awareness, *N'Yata will be pleased that I am having this moment of near-ultimate reality.*

At his stage of development, he could expect to hold on for only a brief time, aligning what was possible for him, setting up as many of the golden lights as he could in the time available. . . . Mustn't waste a second.

One by one the being, himself so small, discharged even tinier bits of the smallness into the dark. Each bit was hard to push away, as if its attachment to him, or consanguinity, prevented it from departing to any distance. The first few yards were tremendously hard, the first miles hard, the first light-years progressively easier, the distance of a galaxy like wafting a feather into a whirlwind. And the dark light-years beyond seemed almost barrierless.

Suddenly, one of the points he had thus put out attracted the being's attention. He thought, *No, oh, no, I mustn't.*

What he fought, then, was a surge of interest within himself in that point. He tried to tell himself the truth—that it was he who had put out the point and it was he who was projecting the interest into it. That it had no interest of its own.

But a curious inversion was taking place—The conviction that the point was of itself interesting, That there was something attractive there, separate from his thought about it.

As he had that awareness, Cemp sensed that the creature's high, pure energy began to drop. Rapidly, it seemed—over how long a period, he didn't know—the being suffered an emotional transformation from a kind of radiance to an . . . oh, well-boredom, through a momentary flash of rage to the self-delusion of, *I am probably god, or at least a subgod. So everything* must *align with me.*

He was back, the creature thought sardonically, to the level of betrayal.

*Well, it was good while it lasted.*

As he had that awareness, he was already *at* the other point, the one that had so automatically aroused his interest.

Every instant that these remarkable events occurred, Cemp was fighting and observing, by means of another aspect of his awareness, a life-and-death battle that had no meaning.

No one was fighting him.

Like a man who falls through an unnoticed manhole into a drainage pipe of deep, dirty, swirling water; like a child grabbing at and abruptly caught by the surging power of a live wire; like someone who puts his foot into a noose, sets off a trigger, and is jerked a hundred feet above ground as a bent tree springs back into position—Cemp had moved himself into a cosmic equivalent of the slipstream of a rocket.

He was instantly beyond his ability to cope . . . struggling with a natural force that transcended his experience. It was a basic condition of space, the existence of which had never been suspected by man or Silkie.

Cemp put up his barriers, drew energy from the trapship, replenished what was being suctioned from him.

The golden dot winked out.

And Cemp grew aware that he was in a large room. Several human beings, who were sitting before an enormous instrument bank, turned and looked at him in amazement.

As Cemp recognized top personnel of the Silkie Authority, Charley Baxter leaped from his chair and came loping across the distances of the thick carpet.

Another realization forced itself upon Cemp—his Silkie body felt unstable in a unique fashion. It was not unpleasant; the sensation was as if some part of him were aware of a distant place.

The alarmed thought came, *I'm still connected to another location. I could be snatched out of here any moment.*

And what was alarming about that was, he had no further defense. Except for one small delaying idea, he had used up his available possibilities.

Accordingly, the real crisis was upon him, unless—

Cemp transformed to human.

Doing so was not a well-considered act. He had the thought that a change of structure might free him even a little from that remote . . . connection. Because it was his only remaining possibility, he made the change at once and, in his haste, half-fell, half-slid to the floor.

The transition, he noted with relief, seemed to have worked. The feeling of being connected faded to a shadowy thing. It was still there but like a whisper in a room where someone had been yelling moments before.

As Charley Baxter came up, Cemp called out to him, "Quick! Let's get to the computer. I don't know what happened. I should be read."

On the way, someone slipped Cemp a robe. He donned it over his naked body without pausing.

There was a little conversation, tense, staccato. Baxter asked, "What seemed to happen?"

"I gained some time," replied Cemp.

As he explained it, it was of course much more than that. Instead of being instantly defeated, he had manipulated and confused the enemy. Confronted by a superior being, he had used what ability and capacity he had. Now, he desperately needed help, some kind of understanding about the fantastic thing he had experienced.

Baxter asked anxiously, "How much time do you think we have?"

Cemp replied, "I have an impression that they're working at top speed. So an hour—no more."

In its swift, electronic way—yet slowly for the urgency Cemp felt—the computer made its study of him and came up with its four alternative answers.

The first of the two that mattered—number three— was strange indeed. "I have the impression," said the computer, "that everything that happened was occurring in someone's mind. Yet there is an impression of something ultimate in that concept. Something . . . well, I don't know . . . really basic to all things."

And of course, that was hard to accept. Ultimate— basic—was too great.

Ultimate, axiomatically, could not be fought or resisted by something less.

"And that," said the computer, "is really all I can tell you. The manipulations of space, of which the Nijjans seem to be capable, are new. It would seem as if the cells in their systems had to adjust to conditions that give them an advantage over other life forms; some kind of greater control over the essence of things."

It was a bad moment. For even as the computer reported failure, Cemp sensed an internal change for the worse. The something out there was adjusting to his human body. He had a sudden conviction that at any moment a threshold point would be crossed.

Hastily, he reported the sensation to Baxter and finished, "I was hoping we'd have time for me to visit the Earth headquarters of the original Silkies, but I'd better go Silkie myself right now."

Charley Baxter's reply showed his awareness of Cemp's danger—the possibility that Cemp might find himself in some far vacuum of space in his unprotected human body. Baxter asked anxiously, "Didn't you transform to human because as a Silkie you were even more vulnerable to whatever is pulling at you?"

It was true. But there was no alternative. As a Silkie he would, temporarily, at least, be safer in a dangerous environment.

Baxter went on, and his voice held a note of strain, "Nat, why don't you change to some other form?"

Cemp turned and stared at him. And then for a space the two of them were silent. They stood there in that plush room, with its cushioned chairs and its small mechanical protrusions—which was all that was visible of the giant computer. Stood there, but finally Cemp said, "Charley, the consequences of what you suggest are an unknown factor."

Baxter said earnestly, "Nat, if we can't trust you to work it out, then it's an unsolvable problem anyway."

The sensation of imminent change was stronger. But still Cemp temporized. What Baxter suggested was almost as world-shaking as the Nijjan threat.

Transform—to anything!

To any body. To any form. Be something entirely different from the three bodies he knew so well.

He believed what Charley had said was a truth. But it was a truth in relation to a known past—the human-Silkie situation that he had grown up with. It was not a truth to someone who didn't have that background. The meteorite "original" Silkie Ou-Dan had made that crystal clear.

Cemp had the strangest conviction of his entire life—that he was like a man poised in pitch darkness on some edge, preparing to jump into the night ahead and below.

It would, of course, be a limited jump. At the moment there were only about three alien changes he could make. He could become a Kibmadine or the creature to which the Kibmadine had changed . . . or a Nijjan.

He explained to Charley, "You have to have a mental picture to go by, have to have 'seen' the other being first; and I have only a few."

"Change to Nijjan!" urged Baxter.

Cemp said, almost blankly, "Are you serious?"

And then, because he had an internal sensation as of something beginning to slip away from him—it was a very distinct impression—he hastily played the Nijjan image, as he had recorded it; "played" it through the transmorpha system.

As he did so, each of his cells received a uniform simultaneous charge of energy that acted like the explosion of the cap of a cartridge, releasing the pent-up energy in the cell.

The transformation was as rapid as it was because the chemical energies thus released needed instantaneous unions with their chemical counterparts.

Again, it was one of those situations where, by theory, the entire process should have required a second or less. In actual fact, of course, living cells were slow to adjust. So it was exactly five and a half seconds after the start that Cemp was in his new state.

He was also, he observed, in a strange place.

# XXVII

CEMP BECAME aware that he was recording the thoughts of the other being again.

This being—the Nijjan enemy—grew conscious of something to his left.

He glanced in that direction and saw that N'Yata had moved from her remote center of being into his space.

It was a movement that he welcomed and admired, since she was at least half a stage above him in development. Under ordinary circumstances, he would have appreciated her coming because it was both flattering to and educational for him. And normally it would have been an ideal opportunity for him to observe and imitate her greater perfection.

But this was not a normal or ordinary occasion. She had come in response to his need for help, his puzzling failure to deal with Cemp.

Her thought about this showed in her movement, and he perceived her as a single golden dot the size of an atom. Her smallness and her location to his left he was able to mark by criss-crossing lines of forces.

Cemp marked it with him, but presently he had a private thought, *How am I observing this?* And then he realized—with his own energy, automatically evoked from him by an emotion that (the other being's thoughts noted with a wry self-judgment) was still only a few vibrations above betrayal.

Once again, logic of levels, with all its implicit awareness of the nature of emotion, was Cemp's only possible overt defense. And of course, as before, betrayal was simply not a tactic by which he could decisively defeat anyone.

Also, he felt intuitively reluctant to trigger the more capable N'Yata to some ultimate level of win.

With these various restrictions in mind, he directed his one defense against all the destruction implicit in the betrayal emotion. Subtly. Urged her to a slightly gayer meaning of betrayal. Suggested seduction. Argued that the pleasure outweighed negative aspects.

His was a skillful counteraction, for the golden dot switched positions in space, moved from his left to directly in front of him.

How many light-years were involved in that switch, Cemp could not determine. For N'Yata was still at a very remote viewpoint, and the vast distances defied measurement by his one-half-step-lower techniques, in which he reflected the condition of the Nijjan body he had duplicated.

*You can still betray!* That was the thought-feeling that flowed back now from the golden dot to Cemp. Having sent the message, the dot began to recede. Cemp felt a distinct drop in his own energy level to a still lower (than betrayal) level, of grief and apathy. As he watched the dot go, the first longing came for death, so great was the outflow of his life energy.

He recognized it as a half-hearted attempt to kill him, sensed that even though she knew he was not the real G'Tono, she was puzzled and that in the final issue, she could not bring herself to destroy another Nijjan, not even a duplicate one.

Her withdrawal was an intent to consider the problem. He felt her let him go. . . .

His thought ended. He was back in the computer room. Cemp glanced over at Baxter and telepathed, "What happened?"

Having asked the question, Cemp grew conscious of three things. The first of these was merely interesting. During Cemp's . . . confrontation with N'Yata, Baxter had moved away.

The man stood now staring at Cemp, a wary expression on his lean face.

Once more, Cemp asked, "I had an experience. What seemed to occur while I was having it?" It was the same question as before, but more detailed.

This time, Baxter stirred. He said aloud, "I don't get your thoughts any more. So let me just say that right now, I sense that your Nijjan body is radiating more force than I can take. Evidently, you're in a different energy state."

Cemp was remembering his own earlier problem in receiving the communication of the Nijjan. After a moment's consideration of the difficulty, he tentatively tried for an adjustment of output in the bank of cells devoted to the problem, and then he telepathed to Baxter, again tentatively.

An expression of relief came over the lean man's face. "Okay," he replied, "we're on. What happened?"

Cemp hastily reported his experience, finishing, "There's no question that my original use of logic of levels confused the first Nijjan I met, whose name I gather is G'Tono. By spiraling him up to a superwin situation, I escaped whatever he had in mind. And now, by becoming a duplicate of him—essentially that's all I did—I momentarily confused N'Yata. But she recovered fast, and so time is of the essence."

"You think—"

"Wait!" admonished Cemp.

The second awareness was suddenly in Cemp's mind, and that was not merely interesting; it was urgent—consciousness of being a Nijjan.

It had all happened so fast. At the moment of change, instant transfer to a confrontation with N'Yata; then back here . . .

Now, Cemp realized that as a Nijjan he could hear sounds. Baxter's human voice had penetrated to him at a normal level—sea-level Earth pressure, it seemed.

With that to start, Cemp did a lightning-swift orientation—not only sound but sight, feeling, proprioceptive sensations; an apparently human physio-emotional spectrum.

And he could walk. He felt odd-shaped appendages that held him, balanced him, enabled him to stand . . . and armlike things, more sinuous.

Cemp was not surprised that he was aware of human qualities. Change of shape was not change of being, but a chameleonlike alteration of appearance—a total alteration as distinct from merely a method of concealment; not simply a blending with a background.

He was the human-Silkie Nat Cemp, in the shape of a Nijjan. His Earth-born cells were the basic stuff of his new body, different undoubtedly from the actual cells of a Nijjan.

Yet the similarity, in its finer details, was sufficiently intricate to be interesting to Cemp. It made him hopeful that by being a Nijjan shape, he would be able also to discover some of the secrets of that shape's abilities.

His attention continued to leap from point to point of his Nijjan body.

The legs and arms—being able to have them in the vacuum of space—that was different from Silkie-human.

The Silkie shape could survive in space only if the interior flesh and structure were separated from the vacuum by a steel-hard chitinous substance. For that, even legs had to be massive. And so Silkies had semilegs and nothing but a grimace where the face and head should be.

The Nijjans evidently had the same ability without change of form. A hard substance? It didn't seem that way. It seemed more like a different molecular structure.

No time to investigate *that!*

On a higher level, there was in the Nijjan body the entire magnetic wave band and radiation sensitivity;

also, awareness of gravity and all the stasis centers that made it possible for Silkies to operate stably in the vacuum of space.

More . . .

Cemp perceived another set of control centers high in the thickest part of the pyramidal shape. But these neural areas were silent, flowed no energy, and responded to none of his hastily directed thought commands.

If there was any automatic activity above the level of mere chemical survival in that mass of nerve substance, Cemp could not detect it.

He surmised uneasily: the space-control lobe of the Nijjan brain? And he had no time to experiment with it. Not yet.

What was particularly frustrating was that there was no larger pyramidal energy image projecting from him. So that was not an automatic process. Could it be an output of some kind from the space-control cells?

No time to investigate that, either—no time, because his third awareness was forcing in upon his attention, and that was something he could do something about.

By his reasoning, furthermore, it was related to the second awareness he had had. Thus, he was not really turning away from what it was like to be a Nijjan to something less urgent. Not completely turning, anyway.

"Wait . . . a little longer," Cemp repeated to Baxter.

Having telepathed the second admonition, Cemp put out another thought on a magnetic beam that a human could read.

The thought was directed toward the Earth headquarters of the space Silkies. It was on an open channel, so he was not surprised when he received answers from three minds, one a Silkie female.

All three answers were the same: "We space Silkies have agreed that we will not discuss our affairs on an individual basis."

"What I have to say is very urgent. Do you have a spokesman?" Cemp asked.

"Yes. I-Yun. But you'll have to come over. He can talk only if some of us are monitoring."

The implication was of group thinking and group action; decisions by many, not merely one. Considering the restrictions—which he did fleetingly—Cemp had a sudden intuition, a thought that was surely an insight of major import.

"I'll be there in . . ." Cemp began.

He paused, turned to Baxter, and asked, "How quickly can you get me over to space Silkie headquarters?"

Baxter was pale. "It would take too long, Nat," he protested. "Fifteen, twenty minutes—"

"In twenty minutes; so get everybody together in one room!" Cemp completed his thought to the Silkies in their distant headquarters.

Whereupon, he mentally persuaded Baxter, still objecting, to literally run to the nearest elevator. People turned and stared as the silvery Nijjan body and the human being ran along side by side. But Cemp was already explaining, already convincing the other.

As a result, what authority could do was done.

A down elevator stopped on an emergency signal, picked them up, and whisked them to the roof. A helijet, about to take off, was held back by a preemptive control-tower command, and presently it was swooping across the rooftops of the huge buildings that made up the Silkie Authority, soaring many degrees indeed away from its original destination.

It zeroed in presently on the landing depot of the three-story building that had been assigned as a preliminary headquarters of the space Silkies.

During the flight, Cemp resumed his magnetic-level communication. He told the receiving trio who the enemy was and explained, "Since I had no reaction to it in my Silkie form, I'm assuming that those of us born on Earth do not have any old reflexes on the subject of Nijjans. But it seemed to me that the meteorite Silkies might."

There was a long pause, and then another mind sent a thought on the magnetic beam. "This is I-Yun. All restrictions are temporarily off. Answer with any truth you have, anyone."

The female Silkie's thought came first. "But it's so many generations ago," she protested. "You believe we'll have an ancestral memory after such a long time?"

Cemp replied, "If that's what it takes, I can only say I hope so, but . . ."

He hesitated. What was in his mind was even more fantastic. He had got the impression from the Glis that a number of really original Silkies were still around.

His brief hesitation ended. He sent the thought.

"You mean, like 100,000 years old?" came an astonished male Silkie response.

"Maybe not that long," said Cemp. "In fact, I compute from feeling-thoughts I recorded that it's not more than 100,000 years since the Glis attached the Silkies to him. But anywhere from 5,000 to 10,000, yes."

There was a pause; then, "What do you expect such a Silkie to do? Defeat a Nijjan? Remember, our understanding is that we Silkies were the ones who were defeated and decimated. And besides, how will we find the old ones? No one remembers anything like that far back; the Glis with its memory-erasing techniques saw to that. Do you have a method of stimulating such ancient reflexes?"

Cemp, who had the perfect, practicable method, wanted to know how many Silkies were in the building at this very moment.

"Oh, about a hundred." That was I-Yun.

It seemed a sizable cross-section. Cemp wanted to know if they were all together as he had requested.

"No, but we'll get them here if you wish."

Cemp very much wished. "And quick!" he urged. "I swear to you that there's no time to waste."

Presently, Cemp sent another magnetic-level message. "Mr. Baxter and I are now landing on the roof. We shall be down in the big room in about one minute."

During that minute he sent streams of thoughts down to the group, explaining his analysis.

The decisive question was, since the Silkies had indeed been decimated in the long ago by the Nijjans, how had a few survived?

Why had not all Silkies been exterminated?

Since the survivors, or their descendants, were the only Silkies available, the answer must be buried deep in their unconscious minds, or else be available by stimulation of ancestral DNA-RNA molecules.

Cemp and Baxter emerged from their elevator and started along a corridor toward a large green door.

At this penultimate moment, I-Yun's thought showed a qualm. "Mr. Cemp," he telepathed uneasily, "we have cooperated with you more than we intended to cooperate with anyone on Earth. But I think we should know before we go any further what—"

At that point, Baxter opened the green door for Cemp, and Cemp walked into the big room.

Cemp was aware that Baxter was returning along the corridor, running at top speed—his retreat was actually protected by an energy screen that Cemp put up at the moment he went through the door. But the agreement was that Baxter would get out of the way, so that Cemp would not have to devote attention to his defense.

Baxter had come this far because he wanted to see the room where the space Silkies were waiting. With that much previsualization, he could get the rest by way of the telepathic channel Cemp left open for him.

In an emergency his experience might be useful. That was the thought. . . .

# XXVIII

At that instant of entry the scene spread before Cemp was of many men and woman, sitting or standing. His Nijjan body had visual awareness to either side, so he also noticed that four Silkie shapes "floated" near the ceiling on both sides of the door. Guards? He presumed so.

Cemp accepted their presence as a normal precaution. His own quick defense against them was to put up a magnetic signal system that, when triggered by any dangerous force, would automatically set up a screen.

The majority of the occupants of the big room were not a prepossessing lot, for the human shape was not easy for these space Silkies. But humanlike they were. And as Cemp entered, they naturally focused their gaze on him.

Every pair of eyes at the exact same moment saw the silvery glittering body of a Nijjan.

How many individuals were present, Cemp did not know or count, then or later. But there was an audible tearing sound as all over the room clothes ripped, threads parted, and cloth literally shredded.

The sound was the result of a simultaneous transformation by the majority from human to Silkie. About a dozen people, eight of them women, merely gasped, made no effort to change.

But—three individuals turned into Nijjans and, having become so, instantly scattered. They ran off in three directions and came to a halt each in a separate corner; they did not actually leave the room.

Cemp waited, tense, all receptors recording, not knowing what more to expect. This was what he had hoped for; and here, in its potentiality, it was. Three. Almost incredibly, three out of a hundred or so had responded with—what? He wanted very much to believe that theirs was an age-old reflex that operated in the presence of Nijjans.

Could it be that the defense against a Nijjan was—to be a Nijjan?

It seemed almost too elementary. Raised numerous questions.

Cemp received a thought from Baxter: "Nat, do you think the old Silkies of long ago might have been killed one by one because they were surprised and couldn't turn Nijjan quickly enough?"

It seemed reasonable. The lag, always that lag in the transmorpha system, had been a dangerous few moments for Silkies.

But the question remained, after turning into Nijjans, what did they know? And what could they do against *real* Nijjans?

Out of the darkness of unknown numbers of millennia, from somewhere below the mist of forgetfulness created by the Glis in its effort at total control, had now come a response. Like a pure light carrying images from a projector, it shone from that far-distant time into the here and now.

Was there more to those images than appeared on the surface? More than the transformation itself?

The swift seconds ran their course, and Cemp got nothing more, nothing special.

Baxter's anxious mind must have registered Cemp's developing disappointment, for his thought came, "Isn't there some association they've got with the changeover, some reason why the transformation was successful?"

Cemp took that thought, made it his own, transferred it to a magnetic wave, and sent it on to the three Silkie-Nijjans.

With that, he got his first nonautomatic response.

Said one, "You want my moment-by-moment reactions? Well, the reflex that was triggered had only an ordinary transmorpha lag. I estimate no more than seven Earth seconds was what the changeover required. While waiting for the change, and immediately after, my impulse was to escape—but of course, I only ran a few yards and then recognized that you were not a true Nijjan. At which moment of awareness I stopped my flight. There followed intense anxiety—memories, obviously, since I had no reason to feel any of that here. But that's it."

Cemp asked quickly, "You had no impulse to use any attack or defense energies?"

"No, it was just change and get out of there."

One of the remaining two Nijjan-Silkies was able to add only a single new thought. "I had the conviction," he said, "that one of us was doomed, and I felt sad and wondered who it would be this time."

"But there was nothing," Cemp persisted, "about *how* one of you would be killed and, I presume, no awareness of the means by which the Nijjan had suddenly appeared in your midst without advance warning?"

"Nothing at all," answered the three in unison.

Baxter's third thought intruded. "Nat, we'd better get back to the computer."

En route, Baxter made another, more farreaching decision.

Preceded by a private emergency code known for its extreme meaning only to its recipients, he mentally projected by way of a general-alarm system in the Silkie Authority a warning message to "all Silkies and all Special People"—slightly more than six thousand persons. . . .

In the warning Baxter described the Nijjan danger and the only solution so far analyzed for Silkies—change to Nijjan and scatter!

Having completed his own message, Baxter introduced Cemp, who broadcast for Silkies only the Nijjan image.

Shortly after, Baxter and Cemp completed their trip to the computer, which said, "Though these new data give no additional clue to the space-control methods of the Nijjans, we can now view the nature of the battle by which the old Silkie nation was gradually decimated. The method was a cautious, never-altered system of one-by-one extermination."

The computer thought it interesting that even the higher-type Nijjan female N'Yata had not made a serious attempt to kill Cemp while he was in his Nijjan form.

Listening to the analysis, Cemp was plunged into gloom. It was clear now that, first, the Glis molecule, and then his small use of logic of levels on betrayal, had saved him in his first two encounters.

He wondered blankly, what *could* be the nature of space that man or Silkie had never so much as dreamed of?

... Nothing to something to nothing, and that slightly caved-in—collapsed—body of Lan Jedd; these were the only clues.

"Space," said the computer in answer to Cemp's question, "is considered to be an orderly, neutral vastness wherein energy and matter masses may interact according to a large but finite number of rules. The distances of space are so enormous that life has had an opportunity to evolve at leisure in innumerable chance ways on a large but finite number of planets on which—accidentally, it is presumed—suitable conditions developed."

The definition deepened Cemp's gloom. It seemed like truth. Yet if it was literally so, then how could the Nijjan have spanned those enormous distances in apparently no time at all? One or more of the assumptions needed to be modified. Or so it seemed.

Cemp said unhappily, "We've got to remember we're looking at an evolved universe. Perhaps, in its younger days, space was less—what did you say?—neutral. The speculative question arises, what might an unorderly space have been like?"

"This is something that can be learned, now that logic of levels is applicable."

"Eh!" That was Baxter, astounded. "Logic of levels will work here? How?"

"Consider!" said the computer. "A command to operate the space-control areas will have to come from the central self of a Nijjan. Our problem is, we don't know what that command is, but some kind of thought stimulates it. Once it is stimulated, a basic action response occurs. Naturally, someone will have to force a dangerous confrontation in order to trigger such a cycle."

Cemp said quickly, "Do you still have the feeling that what we might trigger is bigger than what happened to the Glis and more basic?"

"Definitely."

"But"—baffled—"what could be bigger than an apparently small object like the Glis expanding into the largest sun in the known universe?"

"This is something you will discover, and I presume you are the one who will discover it."

Cemp, who hadn't thought about it, presumed instantly that he would indeed be the one.

Thinking thus, feeling the irony but resigned nonetheless, Cemp transformed to his Silkie body. He expected that he would immediately perceive the distant tug on all his cells.

But there was nothing. No awareness in him of a faraway segment of space. He had not the faintest sense of being unbalanced at some deep level. His entire body was at peace and in a state of equilibrium with his surroundings.

Cemp reported the situation to Baxter—and then warily transformed to human. But there was no distant pull on him in that state either.

A few minutes later the computer expressed what was already obvious. "They're taking no chances. They never did with Silkies. You'll have to seek them out . . . or else be exterminated one by one, now that they have found you."

From the corner of his eye, Cemp noticed Baxter as that analysis came through. The man's face had a strange look: sort of hypnotic, sort of inward-turning.

Cemp was quick. He grabbed the man and yelled, "What's the thought? What command is being given?"

Baxter twisted weakly in that iron grip, abruptly stopped his resisting, and whispered, "The message I'm getting is absolutely ridiculous. I refuse—"

# XXIX

THE DOORBELL rang with a soft, musical note. Joanne Cemp stopped what she was doing in the kitchen and thought. *The time has come for revelation. The night of no memory is over.*

Having had the thought, casually, as if it were an ordinary concept, she headed for the door. And then she simultaneously realized two things. The shock of each of the two brought a reaction of an intensity that she had not previously experienced in her entire life.

The first realization was, *Night of no memory! . . . Revelation! . . . Why, that's crazy! Where would I get an idea like that?*

The second realization was that she was getting no thoughts from whoever had rung the doorbell.

She felt a chill. She could read minds even better than her Silkie husband by the direct telepathic method. But from the person at the door she perceived no thoughts. It had always been a point of wonder that the Special People were so great in this area of mind reading—something about a unique DNA-RNA combination in the cells of a few human beings that was not duplicated in other humans or in Silkies.

And that ability sensed no presence at the door. Nothing. Not a sound, not a thought, not a sign of another mind or being.

Joanne veered down the hall and into her bedroom and secured her gun. That was pretty weak stuff against what she now suddenly suspected might be a space Silkie woman making a second visitation. But the first Silkie woman had not been mentally silent.

Still, against a human the gun would be effective,

particularly since she had no intention of opening the door. A moment later, Joanne turned on the closed-circuit TV and found herself gazing at—nothing.

She had the thought: The bell was rung from a distance, from many light-years away, to tell you that someone will come. You have done your duty. The painful laboratory change from Nijjan to human will now be reversed. . . . Unfortunate that Nijjans have had no natural way of transforming from one shape to another. However, by changing shape in this difficult way you were enabled to marry an Earth Silkie. By so doing you have lulled him and understand him; and now that the space Silkies have finally revealed themselves, we can finally decide what to do with this dangerous race; and what you and the other Special People have done will determine the fate of these universe endangerers.

Joanne frowned at the message, but she made no answer; she simply stood there silent and disturbed. What kind of nonsense! . . .

The thought went on, You are skeptical, no doubt, but it will soon be proved, and you may now ask any questions you wish.

After many heartbeats, during which Joanne considered, remembered, decided, she still refused to reply.

She saw the message as a trap, a lie, an attempt to locate her if she replied. Actually, even if it was true, it didn't matter. *Her* involvement on Earth was total. She thought to herself, *This is the final Silkie-Nijjan confrontation, and it's all a bunch of Nijjan madness.*

She didn't have to accept such a solution, no matter if her own background was Nijjan.

During all these intense moments, Joanne had kept her own thoughts out of the telepathic band. Yet the fear was already in her, the realization that this message, or a variation of it, was probably being received by all 4,700-odd Special People on Earth. And the fear that almost petrified her was that among these numerous persons, somebody would be foolish, somebody would answer.

The awful conviction came that any reply would mean disaster for everybody, because all the Special People without exception knew *so much* that was basic about Silkies.

Even as she had the anxiety, somebody did answer. Two women and three men almost simultaneously projected their outraged replies, and Joanne received every nuance of the emotion that accompanied each unwise reply.

Said one, "But many of the Special People have died in the past two hundred years."

A second chimed in, "So they can't be immortal Nijjans."

A third mind said, "If what you say is true, it proves that Silkies and Nijjans could live together."

The fourth person—a man—was scornful. "This time you crazy killers have run up against more than you bargained for."

And the fifth telepathic human reply to the Nijjan trap was, "I don't know what you expect to gain from this lie, but I reject it."

That was as far as the doomed five got with their response. The best later reconstruction of what happened then was—in each instance, answering located the individual to the remote watching minds of the Nijjans. At once a Nijjan arrived on the scene—in the house, on the street, wherever—and seized the person.

At the moment of seizure a single mental scream of despairing realization came from one of the women. The remaining four went silently to their fates.

What had happened was this: Shortly after the space Silkie Ou-Dan left Cemp in the ship near the dead body of Lan Jedd, he saw a rapid movement beside him. That was all Ou-Dan had time to observe. The next split instant he was subjected to an internal pressure against which he had no defense. It could have been his moment of death, for he was completely surprised and helpless. But the Nijjan G'Tono, having already had his double failure with Nat Cemp, wanted a prisoner and not a dead body. Not yet.

Moments later, he had the unconscious Ou-Dan on his own planet.

The resultant study of the internal workings of a Silkie was somewhat disappointing to the various Nijjans who came from distant places to look him over. There was nothing in Ou-Dan's memories that explained how Cemp had escaped destruction in his confrontation with G'Tono.

His captors quickly discovered the differences between the space and Earth Silkies and learned from Ou-Dan that Cemp was an Earth Silkie. The Nijjans thereupon reasoned accurately that the space Silkies, being considered unreliable, had simply never been given the secret of the special technique that Cemp had used.

In their study of Ou-Dan, the great beings were delayed for many minutes, perhaps even an entire hour, by an attitude that radiated from him. Ou-Dan so thoroughly dismissed and downrated the human-Silkie relationship that his emotion about it was a barrier. Thus, for a decisive time, the Nijjans did not note in his mind that the Special People were a unique human group.

During that vital period, Baxter extended the information about the Nijjans to the Special People, and Cemp and he met with the space Silkies and talked to the computer. And so, when the five Special People were captured, Earth was as ready as it would ever be.

The Nijjans secured the basic clue from all five of their human prisoners. Moments later, the knowledge of logic of levels was going down the Nijjan line of planets, multimillions of them.

# XXX

On G'Tono's planet was a tall mountain that rose thousands of feet sheer from the ground. On top of that mountain stood the palace of G'Tono.

Inside the throne room, the octopus people hurried and bustled and shuffled in a steady stream of activity, partly ritual and partly in relation to the five human prisoners and to the space Silkie Ou-Dan.

The quintet of Special People were beginning to feel a little easier; they were no longer so certain that they would be murdered out of hand. Ou-Dan, who had been internally damaged as a result of his interrogation, lay unconscious in one corner, ignored by all except a few guards.

Across the room from the humans—a distance of more than a hundred yards—was a great, glittering throne. On the throne sat a figure even more glittery in his natural state than any of the inanimate objects that framed him—G'Tono himself!

About a dozen of the octopus people lay face down on the marble in front of their tyrant. Their gentle, bulbous faces pressed against the hard floor. It was a priceless privilege for those who were there, and every half hour the dozen or so personages reluctantly gave up their places to another group of the same size, all of whom were equally appreciative.

G'Tono paid no attention to these, his servant people. He was engaged in a mental conversation with N'Yata 2,400 light-years away, and the subject of their concern was the fate of the prisoners.

G'Tono believed that the five Special People and Ou-Dan had served their purpose and should be put to

172

death on the betrayal principle. N'Yata felt that no final decision should be made about prisoners until the Earth Silkie situation was entirely resolved, which could happen only if all the Silkies were destroyed.

She pointed out that the betrayal idea did not apply except where it was part of a control system. No control existed yet for human beings, and none would exist until a Nijjan took over Earth as his domain.

G'Tono was beginning to feel very boldly masculine in relation to N'Yata. So he took the attitude that her answer showed a lovable feminine weakness, a caution unnecessary now that the human-Silkie problem was solved. For all Nijjan purposes, he felt, the procurement of the logic-of-levels concept ended the danger.

"You seem to believe that something can still go wrong," he protested.

"Let's wait," said N'Yata.

G'Tono replied scathingly that Nijjans, after all, had their own rationality, long-tested by experience. It was not necessary to await the outcome of a logical sequence once it had been reasoned through.

He thereupon listed for N'Yata the reasons why the Silkies were defeated for all practical purposes. Nijjan attacks, said G'Tono, would in the future be made in such a way that no Silkie could ever again hitch a ride as the Silkie Cemp had so skillfully done. Furthermore, the vast majority of Nijjans, though allowing through their mind barriers the information about logic of levels, had fortunately refused to be involved in the actual struggle.

G'Tono explained, "Contrary to our initial irritation with their refusal to participate, what they have done— or rather, not done—is really favorable to our side." He broke off for purposes of clarifying his point. "How many helpers do we have?"

"You saw most of them," N'Yata answered. "About a hundred."

The smallness of the number momentarily gave pause to G'Tono. He had a natural cynicism about things Nijjan; yet his rationalization seemed true to him. It was true that Nijjans had a hard time getting along with one another. So *many* proud individuals, each with his planet—of which he or she was absolute master. Where everyone without exception was a king or a queen, egos had a tendency to soar out of sight.

Once in a while, of course, a queen would accept a communication from a king, as N'Yata had done with him. And at certain times kings were receptive to a communication from a queen. G'Tono had observed with jealousy that the hundred-odd who had responded to N'Yata's call for volunteers were all males.

But that very aloofness of the great majority was now, G'Tono argued, a sign of the indestructibility of the Nijjan race. Scattered all over the universe, out of contact with their own kind, individual Nijjans in their total numbers couldn't be hunted down in a million years, even assuming that somebody existed with the ability and power to kill Nijjans; but there was no such person, group, or race.

"And now that we have the only dangerous Silkie weapon, logic of levels, our position is absolutely impregnable," G'Tono pointed out.

N'Yata replied that she was still studying logic of levels and that it wasn't the mistakes Nijjans might make in the future that worried her; indeed, she conceded that the chance of additional errors was unlikely. The question was, could G'Tono and she recover from the errors that had already been made?

G'Tono was astonished. "The only mistake that would matter," he objected, "would be if we had left this Silkie Cemp some means of forcing me or you to transport him here by our space-control system. Though I," he continued scornfully, "would certainly like to be the first to know of such a method, I find myself wondering, would he dare to come? Because what could he do in a direct confrontation with me, who is basically more powerful than any Silkie?"

He had been thinking hard while he was speaking, and now he saw an opening in her logic and a way of gaining his own point.

"As I see it," he said, "the one way in which we might be vulnerable is through these prisoners. So I think you will agree that instant extermination is a safety precaution, if nothing more. Don't try to interfere!"

He did not wait for N'Yata's reply but sent a high-level energy blast at the two women and three men and at the helpless Ou-Dan. All six prisoners were literally dissolved into their component elements; death was as rapid as that.

Having taken the action, G'Tono proceeded with his listing of favorable points. "After all," he said, "lacking space control, Silkies are trapped on or near Earth or at best are subject to the slow speeds of ordinary space travel. I estimate that in three Earth weeks I could perhaps expect to have an Earth ship arrive at my planet, whereupon if you were to invite me, I could visit you for a while. And frankly, what could they do? Where could they look? A Nijjan can disappear into distance in a split instant—"

He broke off, feeling suddenly dizzy.

N'Yata telepathed sharply, "What's happening?"

"I—" faltered G'Tono.

That was as far as he got. The dizziness had become an all-enveloping madness, and he fell from his throne to the marble floor—fell hard, rolled over onto his back, and lay there like one dead.

# XXXI

THE NIJJANS had lied; that was what snatched Cemp's most intense interest.

A quick check of records by the computer had established with thousands of detailed documentations that the Special People could not possibly have been Nijjans.

It was hard to believe that the Nijjans could have exposed one of their number to a counterattack on that level. But it looked as if they had.

Cemp shared his analysis with Charley Baxter and watched Baxter become excited. The thin man said, "You're right, Nat. A lie is a complete disaster in a world where people understand the energy flows involved and can control them, as Silkies can."

. . . Because an existing object is truth incarnate. There it is—whatever it is—unparadoxical, without an opposite.

It cannot not-be. Or at least, it cannot not-have-been; if it was matter and has been converted to energy, or vice versa, it still exists in some aspect of its ever-form.

A lie about such an object is a mental attempt to alter the "is" of it. Basically, the effort implicit in the lie is to create a dichotomy where none can exist. There is no opposite; yet the lie says there is.

Hence, the moment a dichotomy is evoked in somebody's mind, a confusion is simultaneously created.

It was too potentially great a possibility to miss.

In telling his plan to Baxter, Cemp pointed out, "You'll have to send a ship after me, because I'll be stranded there."

"You don't think the method of getting you to Nijja will also get you away?" Baxter asked doubtfully.

"No, somebody will be riding herd on all this, and they'll notice."

"It'll take three weeks for a ship to get there," Baxter objected.

Cemp couldn't take the time to consider that. The pace of this battle was superspeed. Since the struggle had begun out there between G'Tono and himself, the enemy had taken time only to make brief studies of new data before striking again.

After all," said Cemp, "I can't be sure how successful I'll be. I expect to get whoever told the lie, but that won't solve the problem. And I'll set it up so that whoever helps him is doomed also. But a chain reaction like that can go only so far before somebody gets wise."

Baxter spoke again, urgently. "Now that these beings have logic of levels, they'll be able to trigger it in you even as you're triggering it in them. Have you thought of that?"

Since there was no defense against logic of levels, Cemp hadn't even considered it. There being no point in thinking about it, now that it had been called to his attention . . . he didn't. He converted to Nijjan and projected the thought "I want you to recall the moment when the message arrived telling you the lie that you were a Nijjan."

Between such experts as Baxter and himself, it required less than a minute to make a study of the wave patterns and to measure the subtle variations of the Nijjan version of the telepathic band of the Special People —and to superimpose on that exact band and that individual variation *all* two hundred and seventy-eight dichotomies, known to be the most confusing of the verbal opposites that had mentally tangled human beings since the beginning of language.

*Right-wrong . . . good-bad . . . justice-injustice*— a living brain receiving for the first time such a madness in the time of a few seconds could go into a state of total confusion.

At key points along that train of words, Cemp placed large, hypnotic-type command loads designed to influence the receiving Nijjan brain during the confusion: first to utilize Cemp's own previous experience to transport him through space; and, second, to set up a basic logic of levels in the receiving Nijjan brain. . . .

Cemp arrived—it was part of his hypnotic command to G'Tono—outside the atmosphere of G'Tono's planet. As he descended toward the surface, he saw there was a great city below and a huge ocean beside it.

He landed on an isolated beach of that ocean where the thunder of the surf and the smell of the sea briefly enticed him. Ignoring that sudden desire for the feel of water, he walked toward the city. At the outskirts, he boldly entered the first of the odd-shaped dwellings he came to—odd in that the doorways were low and broad, and inside he had to stoop because the ceilings were less than six feet high. There were three chunky octopus-like aliens inside. But he saw them; they never saw him. Cemp manipulated the hallucinatory mechanisms of the three, whereupon they observed him as one of themselves. After studying their minds, Cemp carefully went to a nearby street, climbed up to a roof, and watched the octopus beings who went by.

As Cemp had already correctly analyzed, these beings were not dangerous to him, and they were very definitely not up to defending themselves. After reading the minds of several hundreds, Cemp did not detect a single suspicious thought. The fundamental goodness of the beings he observed decided him on his next move.

Minutes later, he walked in on several leading members of the government, hallucinated them into seeing him as a human being, and thought at them, "Where is the one who can betray?"

The tense creatures had drawn away from him. They

did not understand the significance of his question, for they said that on Nijja no one ever betrayed anyone.

The answer amused Cemp in a steely-grim fashion. It meant, as he had suspected, that there was only one betrayal cycle in action on the entire planet—the true Nijjan as the betrayer and all these beings who must conform.

He directed another thought. "Has this planet always been called Nijja?"

They knew of only one other name. Anthropological studies of their antiquity indicated that at the time the common language had begun, some indeterminate thousands of years before, the name had been Thela, meaning Home of the Brave. Nijja, on the other hand, in their language meant Home of the Pure.

Obviously, the name would have to have a meaning in their language as well as in that of the true Nijjans. A different meaning, of course.

"I see," said Cemp.

And he did see.

With that, he asked one more question. "Where can I find the one who requires purity?"

"Oh, you can see him only through the police."

*Where else?* thought Cemp to himself sarcastically.

Whereupon, the exact, proper time having gone by and the exact moment for G'Tono to awaken having come, he directed a thought on the Special People telepathic band. "I am that Silkie who confronted you after you killed my Silkie associate—and I'm sure now it was *you* who killed him. As I now understand it, this planet illustrates what you meant when you stated that Nijjans had no home planet in the ordinary sense. *All* planets controlled by a Nijjan are part of the Nijjan system—the nearest place, in other words, where a single ruling Nijjan could be located. Is that correct?"

Along with the message, Cemp projected the thought that would trigger the logic-of-levels cycle he had set up in G'Tono's brain. Having done so, Cemp spoke again to the focal point nearly three hundred miles away. "You'd better talk to me before it's too late."

Moments after that, Cemp sensed a peculiar sensation in his transmorpha system—N'Yata, he thought. He remembered Baxter's fear that he, too, might be attacked, and here it was. It interested him intensely to observe that it was the mechanism for changing form that was affected; it was not surprising, really, but nobody had known. By the time he had that thought, he had already accepted his personal disaster. From the beginning he had had to consider himself expendable.

Cemp felt briefly sad for Joanne. He presumed that he would die, and her life would now have to go on without him. As for what might happen to the Nijjans . . . Cemp felt a chill, recalling what the computer had predicted—that the Nijjan logic of levels would be bigger than what had happened to the Glis.

Again he wondered, *What could be bigger than that?* The awareness remained with him only fleetingly. Abruptly, he didn't have time to consider anything except what was happening to him.

# XXXII

For Cemp, there was, first of all, a kaleidoscope of visual images.

He saw Nijjan bodies and faces—if the upper part of the pyramidal shape could be considered a face. The images streamed by, not exactly silently, for thoughts came from some of them.

Cemp himself seemed to be floating along in a timeless void, for each set of Nijjan thoughts came to him separate and distinct:

"But how did he do it?"

"What exactly is happening?"

"Why not kill him and then solve the problem ourselves?"

"Because we don't even know what part of the Nijjan brain was utilized for the attack, that's why. Besides, we have no proof yet that we can kill him. In this Silkie, logic of levels seems to be a time phenomenon. In us, it's of course the space thing."

As these thoughts and others like them whispered into Cemp's awareness, he was conscious of a developing stir in the greater distance of the Nijjan world. Other minds, at first a few, then many, then tens of thousands, turned their attention in amazement and took note of him and had *their* thoughts . . . and were hooked into G'Tono's disaster.

Like an anthill into which somebody has kicked deeply, the Nijjan system began to roil and churn with innumerable reactions. What they were afraid of briefly held Cemp's astonished interest—two bodies cannot occupy the same space or two spaces the same body; there was danger that this would now happen.

181

More basic, the space-time continuum, though it was a self-sustaining mechanism of immense but finite complication, needed Nijjans to survive—*that* was the thought. So that if a Nijjan were overstimulated, space might have a reaction.

That was how Lan Jedd had been killed—a Nijjan consciously overstimulating himself had in some small, precise way elicited a reaction in the space occupied by Lan's body.

Push at the universe, at space. A Nijjan might be affected. Push at a Nijjan; the universe would push back or adjust to the push in some fundamental way.

*What are they implying?* thought Cemp, staggered. *What are they saying?*

Between the universe and the Nijjans a symbiotic relation. If one was unstable, so was the other. And the Nijjans were becoming unstable.

As Cemp's awareness reached that point, there was a flash of alarmed agreement that extended through every observing Nijjan mind. Whereupon, N'Yata telepathed to Cemp, "I speak for Nijja. We're in the process of being destroyed by a chain reaction. Is there anything we can do to save ourselves, any agreement we can make?

"In us," N'Yata continued in that desperate way, "awareness of the connection of life to all atoms in the universe was not dulled. Somehow, in those long-ago days of the beginning of things, we automatically worked out a method of maintaining consciousness without constantly endangering ourselves. Other life forms had to attenuate or shut off direct contact with space and its contents. We Nijjans can therefore be destroyed if we are forced to a state of order from the chaos in which, alone, life can survive, and this forcing you have now done."

It was as far-fetched a story as Cemp had ever heard. "You're a bunch of liars," he said contemptuously, "and the proof is that G'Tono could be victimized by an overflow of opposites.

"The truth is," he went on, "I couldn't believe any promise you made."

There was a pause, brief but pregnant; finally a mental sigh from N'Yata. "It is interesting," she said, resigned, "that the one race we feared above all others—the Silkies—has now made a successful attack on us. Because of the overweening pride of countless Nijjans, we are particularly vulnerable. Each Nijjan, as he tunes in, has a logic-of-levels cycle triggered in him, and there's nothing we can do to warn him ahead of time. What you're saying is, you won't listen to any argument against this."

It was more than that, Cemp saw. Between these two races there was no quick way to cooperation. That would be true, he speculatively realized, even if the fate of the universe depended on it. The Nijjan destruction of Silkies had been too remorseless.

But also, there was really nothing he could do. Logic of levels, once started, could not be interrupted. The cycle would complete in them *and* in him and take whatever course the *logic* required.

A brain mechanism had been triggered. The pattern of that mechanism had been set ages before, and it had no other way to be.

That was as far as his thought had time to go.

There was an interruption. Two things happened, then, almost simultaneously.

From N'Yata's mind to his there leaped an emotion of anguish. "Oh, it's happening," she said.

"What's happening?" Cemp's mind yelled at her.

If there was ever an answer from her, Cemp did not receive it. For at that precise instant he felt a strange, strong feeling inside him.

That was the second event. He was on Earth with Joanne. It was at the beginning of their marriage, and there she was, and there he was, completely real both of them. Outside, the sun was shining.

It grew dark suddenly.

That was earlier, he realized. More than a hundred years before he was born.

*This is the time change in myself,* Cemp thought. Logic of levels affecting *him,* taking him somehow earlier in time, a kind of genetic memory journey.

Night. A dark sky. A Silkie floated silently down from the heavens . . . Cemp realized with a start that that was the first Silkie to come to Earth, the one who, it was later pretended was created in a laboratory.

The scene, so briefly observed, yielded to a view of the city inside the Glis meteorite. There were the space Silkies, and he was there also—or so it seemed. Probably, it was his ancestor with his transmorpha cells—the DNA-RNA memory of earlier bodies.

A space scene came next. A blue-white sun in the distance. Other Silkies around him in the darkness. A contented happiness was in all of them.

Cemp had an impression that the time was long ago indeed, twenty or more thousand Earth years, before contact with Nijjans.

Now, a more primitive scene showed. Millions of years earlier, his impression. Something—himself, but different, smaller, less intelligent, more creaturelike—clung to a small rock in space. Darkness.

Another scene. Billions of years. And not darkness but brightness. Where? Impossible to be sure. Inside a sun? He vaguely suspected, yes.

It was too hote. He was flung in a titanic eruption of matter into the far blackness.

Flung earlier.

As he receded to an even remoter time, Cemp felt himself somehow still connected to G'Tono and to the other Nijjans, somehow held to what, for want of a better understanding, he decided was a mental relationship.

Because of that tenuous mind connection and interaction, he was able to sense the Nijjan disaster from a safe distance in time.

It was possible, then, that he was the only living being who, from his vantage point, witnessed the destruction of the eight-billion-light-year-in-diameter universe, of which Earth's galaxy was but one small bit of cosmic flitter.

# XXXIII

THE START of it was very similar to when the betrayal-win cycle in G'Tono had been triggered toward ultimate win during his second confrontation with Cemp.

Swiftly, there came the moment when all those connected Nijjan bodies reached the dividing line between becoming ultrasmall or superlarge. But this time the victims had no choice. Winning was not involved. It was a logic-of-levels cycle, in its ultimate meaning, operating on and through innumerable individuals, each of whom had the potential for that ultimate state.

Every rock has in it the history of the universe; every life form has evolved from a primitive state to a sophisticated one. Touch the wellspring of that evolution in a living thing—or a rock—and *it has to remember.*

For the millions of Nijjans, it was the end. The process that was happening to them was not concerned with maintaining identity.

One moment each Nijjan was a unit object, a living being, with location and mass; the next, the Nijjan brain center that had the ability to move the individual Nijjan through space tried to move him simultaneously into all spaces. Instantly, the entire Nijjan race was shredded into its members' component atoms.

On the object level, the process scattered them, put one atom here, another there, quadrillions more in an many places.

At the moment when all Nijjans became as large as the universe, the universe inverted, in relation to them, to its real normalcy, to the perfect order that is inherent in a dot the size of an atom, which is unaffected by other atoms.

It was not a shrinking phenomenon. Turning inside-out was the best analogy. The collapse of a bubble.

Cemp, who was merely tuned in to G'Tono and the others, felt his own thought expand with the doomed Nijjans to a state that was in exact proportion to the size of the universe with which the Nijjans had interacted.

Having become, in this purely mental way, larger than space and time, Cemp mentally blinked away his dizziness and looked around him. At once he saw something in the great dark. He was distracted, and he forgot the dot that had been the universe.

It thereupon disappeared.

The tiny spot of light, the universe, which one moment had glowed with such brilliance, winked out and was gone.

Cemp was aware of its vanishment with a portion of his mind, but he could not immediately turn his attention away from the sight that had made him forget.

He was looking at the "tree."

He was at such a remote viewpoint, at such a vastness in relation to all things, that, yes, he saw the golden tree.

Presently, he forced himself to look away from that jeweled thing.

When Cemp finally, after what seemed to be several seconds, was able to consider the disappearance of the universe once more, he thought, *How long has it been gone? A thousand, a million, a trillion years or no time at all?*

Perhaps, in some future when he reached this viewpoint, not by artificial projection, but by growth, he would be able to count the time elaspsed in such a phenomenon.

He was still thinking about it, bemused, when he

felt an instability in his position. He thought, *Oh-oh, I'm going to invert again.*

The first evidence of his unstable state was that the glorious tree disappeared. Realization came that he probably had only moments to find the universe.

How do you find a universe?

As Cemp discovered, then, it was not really a problem. The entire meaning of logic of levels was based on the certainty that all life forms at some inner root know the origin of things and that by the very nature of their structure they are balancing themselves against all other things.

There is no moment when the tiniest insect or plant or rock or grain of sand is not interacting. The atoms at the centers of remote stars are part of that interaction.

The problem is not whether the interaction is happening. The problem is that if one is to function, his awareness of many things had to be reduced.

Such attenuation is not normally conscious. Hence, sensitivity to many good things is automatically cut down so close to zero that in this universe, apparently only the Nijjans had retained, through all the vicissitudes of their evolution, the cellular method of space awareness and control.

As Cemp remembered his universe, it began to interact with him, to become in essence what he knew it to be. And there it suddenly was, a dot of golden brightness.

Cemp sensed by the interaction he continued to feel that it was still re-forming deep inside itself, responding exactly to his universal memory of it. He had a mighty thought: *Before it all reverts to exactly the way it was, why don't I change it?*

Obviously, there was no time for detailed consideration. A few flash thoughts, quick judgments, snap decisions—and that would be it. It was never or now. Forever.

The Nijjans?

In a way, he could understand that they had felt it necessary to protect themselves and the space-time continuum by destroying races that were capable of challenging Nijjan hegemony. So they were not as guilty as he had once considered them. But the truth was, the universe did not need a race that could destroy it. It was time the place became permanent.

Cemp refused to remember the Nijjans in his recollection of the plenum.

So what about human beings, the Special People, and the space Silkies?

Cemp's immediate solution—in his universe they *all* became Earth Silkies with the ability to change to any form and a complete willingness to play a benevolent police role everywhere in space.

And without exception, they understood the Nijjan method of space control, but their ability to interact with space was on the small scale necessary for transportation. In addition, no Silkies were subject to logic of levels, and all the effects of the cycle that had been triggered in him were reversed. Also, in case there was any question, Silkies were immortal.

There was no Kibmadine race—Cemp felt no mercy for those perverted creatures.

And Earth was back with her own sun.

Was it a good way for things to be? There was no one to say him yea or nay. He thought it, and then it was too late to remember it differently.

In a flash, the orderly perfection of the single light in the blackness . . . altered, expanded. As Cemp watched tensely, the ocher-colored dot reached the moment of inversion.

For Cemp, it was the return to smallness. Something grabbed him, did an irresistibly powerful thing with him, squeezed him—and pushed.

When he could perceive again, the starry universe stretched around him in every direction.

He realized he was somewhere in space, his Nijjan body intact. For that supersensitive shape and form, now that he understood it, orientation in space was an instinct. Here he was; *there* was Earth. Cemp did the Nijjan space-control manipulation and interacted with another space many light-years distant whose existence he sensed. With that space Cemp did the inversion process on a small scale, became a dot, became himself, became a dot . . . something to nothing to something. . . .

And he stepped 80,000 light-years into the Silkie Authority and said to Charley Baxter, "Don't bother sending that ship after me. I won't be needing it."

The thin man gazed at him, eyes shining. "Nat," he breathed, "you've done it; you've won."

Cemp did not reply immediately. There was a question in his mind. Since, while the universe was being destroyed and reborn, he had been in a time change, had he witnessed and participated in the second formation of the continuum?

*Or the first?*

He realized it was a question to which he would never know the answer.

Besides . . . could it all have been a fantasy, a wish that drifted through his mind while he was unconscious, the strangest dream ever?

There was a great window to his right, a massive structure that led to a balcony from which a Silkie could launch himself. Cemp walked out onto the balcony.

It was night. Earth's old moon floated in the dark sky above, and there were the familiar star configurations he knew so well.

Standing there, Cemp began to feel excitement, a surging consciousness of the permanence and finality of his victory.

"I'm going to Joanne," he announced to Charley Baxter, who had come up behind him.

As Cemp launched himself into the familiar universe that was Earth, he was thinking: He had great things to tell his darling.

## ACE RECOMMENDS . . .

| | |
|---|---|
| **THE BROKEN LANDS**<br>by Fred Saberhagen | 08130 — 50¢ |
| **THE MOON OF GOMRATH**<br>by Alan Garner | 53850 — 50¢ |
| **MOONDUST**<br>by Thomas Burnett Swann | 54200 — 50¢ |
| **THE SILKIE**<br>by A.E. Van Vogt | 76500 — 60¢ |
| **OUT OF THE MOUTH OF THE DRAGON**<br>by Mark S. Geston | 64460 — 60¢ |
| **DUNE**<br>by Frank Herbert | 17260 — 95¢ |
| **MEN ON THE MOON**<br>Edited by Donald A. Wollheim | 52470 — 60¢ |
| **THE WARLOCK IN SPITE OF HIMSELF**<br>by Christopher Stasheff | 87300 — 75¢ |
| **THE YELLOW FRACTION**<br>by Rex Gordon | 94350 — 60¢ |
| **THE MERCY MEN**<br>by Alan E. Nourse | 52560 — 60¢ |
| **THE REBEL OF RHADA**<br>by Robert Cham Gilman | 71065 — 60¢ |

Available from Ace Books (Dept. MM), 1120 Avenue of the Americas, New York, N.Y. 10036. Send price of book, plus 10¢ handling fee.